Marni cleared her throat, beginning to speak louder this time. "Listen, I'm going to give you exactly sixty seconds to gather your clothes and get out of this house!"

"Ay. Dios!" A sharp male voice exploded in her ears. Definitely not the voice of a teenager. A string of sharp Italian curse words followed.

Nope. That was no kid.

In fact, the voice sounded all too familiar. Marni's blood turned to ice in her veins. It couldn't be. But the next word she heard only confirmed that indeed it could.

"Gattina? Is that you?"

Oh no. There was only one person who ever called her that. But how? Why? With great reluctance, Marni lowered her palm from her eyes and fearfully opened her lids.

She'd been so wrong. There was no couple on the bed. Just one solitary man. To her horror, he happened to be no other than Gio Santino. Her best friend Nella's brother. The same man she'd had a crush on for most of her life.

Well, at least she'd been right about one thing. The intruder was indeed undressed.

Dear Reader,

Oftentimes, the person we are toughest on is ourselves. Self-forgiveness does not come easy for most people. In the wake of a serious mistake, one that might have caused harm to others, we often don't afford ourselves much grace or charity.

Such is the case with Gio Santino. He's made a terrible error in judgment, one that has led to intensive damage not only to himself but also to another. He doesn't feel worthy of forgiveness, or understanding, or—least of all—love.

But both redemption and love are bestowed on him by a most unexpected source, his little sister's best friend. Gio has known Marni most of his life, didn't dare think of her as anything more than a family friend. Much to his surprise, she turns out to be the path toward atonement he didn't think he was worthy of. It takes Marni to show Gio how to forgive himself as she overcomes her own past missteps.

Along the way, they fall hopelessly in love with each other. I hope you enjoy their path.

Nina

Two Weeks to Tempt the Tycoon

—

Nina Singh

Recycling programs
for this product may
not exist in your area.

ISBN-13: 978-1-335-73712-0

Two Weeks to Tempt the Tycoon

Copyright © 2023 by Nilay Nina Singh

Harlequin Enterprises ULC
22 Adelaide St. West, 41st Floor
Toronto, Ontario M5H 4E3, Canada
www.Harlequin.com

Printed in U.S.A.

Nina Singh lives just outside Boston, Massachusetts, with her husband, children and a very rambunctious Yorkie. After several years in the corporate world, she finally followed the advice of family and friends to "give the writing a go, already." She's oh-so-happy she did. When not at her keyboard, she likes to spend time on the tennis court or golf course. Or immersed in a good read.

Books by Nina Singh

Harlequin Romance

How to Make a Wedding

From Tropical Fling to Forever

Their Festive Island Escape
Her Billionaire Protector
Spanish Tycoon's Convenient Bride
Her Inconvenient Christmas Reunion
From Wedding Fling to Baby Surprise
Around the World with the Millionaire
Whisked into the Billionaire's World
Wearing His Ring till Christmas
Caribbean Contract with Her Boss

Visit the Author Profile page at Harlequin.com.

To all those with the grace and heart to forgive.

CHAPTER ONE

THERE WAS SOMEONE else here in the house with her. Maybe more than one someone.

Marni Payton's heart slammed against her chest as she shut the wooden door behind her. It had been unlocked. This was so not the welcome she'd been expecting after a long, turbulent flight and an exhausting day of travel.

But she had a more pressing matter at the moment.

Nella had warned her there might be squatters at the villa this time of year. She'd said they were usually harmless. Older kids, mostly, who were looking for a place to party. Teenagers trying to get away from under the watchful eyes of strict parents.

Which, on the surface, did sound harmless enough. Or at least it had when Nella had explained it to her a month ago, while offering Marni the use of her beachside villa in Capri for two weeks before she and her husband would need it back.

Now, however, the knowledge did little to calm Marni down. Shaking with fear, she stood in the middle of the foyer, listening to the sounds coming from upstairs. What if it wasn't a bunch of kids up there? What if the house was being robbed? Or she was about to be attacked?

Marni stepped backward, readying to flee the house, her gaze still locked to the top of the stairs. She reached for the cell phone in her back pocket to call the authorities. In her fear and panic, she yanked it out too jerkily and dropped it to the tile floor. It fell with a loud crashing sound and she watched in horror as the case popped off and the screen shattered.

So much for calling for help. The taxi that had driven her to the house was long gone. She was on her own. Marni froze in her spot, unable to move or so much as breathe.

Had the intruders heard her dropping her phone? Were they scrambling down right now to come hurt her?

Squeak. Squeak. Squeak.

Oh, God. That was definitely a sound she recognized—the unmistakable noise of the springs in a bed. Whoever was up there was using the very bed she'd be sleeping in! Marni could just guess what they were doing. A wave of indignation rose in her chest. The audacity to break into a house and then do…that! She was as sympathetic as anyone to lovesick teens, but this was miles and miles too far.

It was high time to put a stop to it.

Marni pushed aside her fear in favor of outrage. Plus, they were definitely naked. She had the element of surprise on her side. She'd just go up there, demand they get their clothes on and vacate the premises ASAP. Marni bounded up the stairs before she could change her mind. When she reached the closed bedroom door, she gave a quick knock then covered her eyes before pushing it open. Some things she didn't need to see.

"I won't tell your parents if you both get dressed and leave right now," she said. It was an empty threat. She had no idea who their parents might be or where they lived. "Right now," she repeated.

No answer. Maybe they didn't understand English.

She repeated the bluff in broken Italian. Still nothing. And she didn't hear any scuffling about either.

Of all the nerve. Were they seriously just going to ignore her? At least the squeaking had stopped.

Marni cleared her throat, beginning to speak louder this time. "Listen, I'm going to give you exactly sixty seconds to gather your clothes and get out of this house!"

"Dio!" A sharp male voice exploded in her ears. Definitely not the voice of a teenager. A string of sharp Italian curse words followed.

Nope. That was no kid.

In fact, the voice sounded all too familiar. Marni's blood turned to ice in her veins. It couldn't be. But the next word she heard only confirmed that indeed it could.

"Gattina? Is that you?"

Oh, no. There was only one person who ever called her that. But how? Why? With great reluctance, Marni lowered her palm from her eyes and fearfully opened her lids. She immediately wanted to squeeze them shut again.

She'd been so wrong. There was no couple on the bed. Just one solitary man. To her horror, he happened to be Gio Santino. Her best friend Nella's brother. The same man she'd had a crush on for most of her life.

Well, at least she'd been right about one thing: the intruder was indeed naked.

His usual nightmare had taken quite a surprising turn. Rubbing his eyes, Gio blinked away the grogginess of interrupted sleep and tried to focus on the figure standing at the door.

Yep, it was definitely her. Marni Payton stood

staring at him in shock, wide-eyed, her mouth agape. What in the world was she doing here at his sister's villa in Capri? Marni lived in Boston.

"What are you doing here?" they both asked in unison.

Gio knew what his answer to that question was. He'd been trying to get some much-needed sleep. The insomnia and nightmares were wreaking havoc on him. Not to mention the throbbing pain in his leg and torso.

Marni blinked rapidly before attempting to speak. "Nella said I could stay here. For two weeks. I just arrived."

Huh. Gio ran a hand down his face. "That's funny. Because her husband told me the same thing. That I was welcome to the villa whenever I needed."

Marni swallowed. "Well, clearly there's been some kind of misunderstanding."

"Clearly." He was tempted to throttle Antonella the next time he saw her. As much as he loved her, his sister had always been scattered and disorganized. He didn't know how her new husband dealt with it, for God's sake.

Gio sighed wearily. "Look, we're not going to solve this now." Not that he knew exactly how they *would* solve it at any other time. Other than looking for a hotel room for himself at the earliest opportunity. Which was not going to be easy. Capri was busy with tourists and vaca-tioners this time of year. What a pain.

He was so tired of pain.

"Why don't we go downstairs and talk about this," he offered.

Marni didn't answer for several seconds. He was about to repeat the question when he no-ticed her gaze traveling from his face, past his shoulders, down his chest. Then lower.

She cleared her throat before speaking. "Yeah. Sure. We could do that. But do you mind get-ting dressed first?"

Gio flinched. He totally forgot that he'd climbed into bed completely nude. Much too tired to do more than peel off his gritty clothes before collapsing under the covers. To his hor-ror, he saw the bedsheet and blanket had moved lower below his waist and barely sat on his hips. Reflexively, he yanked the sheet up to below his chest.

"Sure. I can do that," he answered.

"Great. I'll see you in a few," Marni replied, turning on her heel. She shut the door firmly behind her.

Gio leaned back against the pillows and threw his arm over his face. Great. Just great. Not only had his chance at some rest and recu-peration just been soundly ruined, he'd almost flashed his younger sister's dearest friend.

Why did she have to be here? Now of all times? Was nothing going to go his way this year? Guessing he already knew the answer to that question, Gio begrudgingly tossed the covers aside and stood. Pulling his suitcase open, he grabbed a pair of sweats and a T-shirt then made his way down the stairs.

Marni was bent down in the doorway when he got to the first floor. In spite of himself and despite the circumstances, he found himself appreciating the view. The sight of Marni's rounded hips had his mind traveling to places it had no business going.

Whatever she was doing, she was distracted enough that she seemed unaware of him. Hopefully, she hadn't noticed just how long it had taken him to get dressed and get down here. Everything took longer to do these days. Something the doctors kept reminding he'd better get used to.

"What are you doing?" he asked Marni's back.

She straightened and turned to face him, holding something in her hand that might have resembled a cell phone at some point in time.

"I was a little startled when I heard noises upstairs. I panicked and dropped my phone." She held up the object in question and shrugged.

"Noises? What noises?"

"The bed, you were making of lot of racket up there." She pointed to the ceiling. "For someone who was sleeping…" She drifted off and a blush of color rose in her cheeks, her bright hazel eyes grew wide. As if she was embarrassed.

Gio held his hands up, offended and slightly amused at her insinuation. "Marni, it's not like that."

She shook her head, growing redder. "Oh! Of course. Whatever you say. Um… Not that there'd be anything wrong or to be embarrassed about. If that was what you were…doing." She faltered on the last word.

Gio couldn't help chuckling. "Thanks. I guess." What exactly was he thanking her for? "The truth is, I haven't been sleeping well. Lots of tossing and turning. That's if I'm lucky enough to fall asleep in the first place."

She looked unsure of what to say. Best to change the subject. "So you're here on vacation?" he asked.

Marni looked away, but not before he caught a shadow dance across her eyes. "Something like that," she answered.

Huh. He'd thought it was a casual question. But Marni clearly didn't want to talk about what exactly she was doing here, halfway across the world from her home. That suited him just fine.

He didn't really want to get into his own reasons for being here either.

She finally returned his gaze. "Gio. If I'd known you were going to be here, I would have made other arrangements."

"I'd say the same. But we're both here now." The question was, what were they going to do about it?

She glanced around her. "I mean, the place is rather roomy."

Maybe. But there was still only one finished bedroom. And only the one bed. Nella and Alex had never gotten around to furnishing the entire house, having recently purchased it. Gio glanced past the foyer to the sitting area. It looked comfortable enough, but the furniture was hardly ample. He didn't think he'd be able to endure sleeping on the small love seat in the living room. The shape he was in at the moment, his body simply couldn't handle it.

And he wasn't going to ask Marni to sleep there. Old-fashioned or not, his masculine pride simply wouldn't allow it. Which lead to another complication. There was no way he was going to explain to Marni why he wouldn't be able to do the chivalrous thing and sleep on the couch.

"I would call around to see about available hotel rooms, but…" She simply held up her shattered phone to complete the sentence.

"I don't think you'd find one anyway. Places around here are booked months in advance." He rammed his hand through his hair in frustration. "Look. We're not going to solve this now," he repeated. "Why don't you go freshen up and I'll throw a snack together. I don't know about you, but I could use a bite."

As if in answer, her stomach reacted with a low grumble. Gio had to chuckle again. For as long as she and his sister had been friends, she'd always managed to make him laugh. He couldn't even remember the last time he'd laughed since the accident. Marni had been here only a few minutes and he'd already chuckled twice.

Despite the awkward circumstances they found themselves in.

By the time Marni made it back downstairs, Gio had thrown together a rather enticing tray of snacks and munchies, if he did say so himself. He'd loaded the fridge and pantry when he'd gotten here three days ago—it was a rare instance of him planning ahead.

If only he'd lived his life being a better planner. He might be in better physical shape right now, without the throbbing pain in his side and the pronounced limp in his gait. A limp he would have to somehow try to hide now that Marni was here.

He got an appreciative sigh from her when she entered the kitchen and eyed the food tray.

"Wow. You threw together a charcuterie board," she said, then added, "I'm impressed."

A what now? "Uh, thanks, I guess. If you mean the tray of cubed cheese, tapenade, meat and grapes. Where I come from, we call it antipasto."

She smiled wide. "Whatever you want to call it, sure beats the dry granola bars I have stashed in my purse. A man of many talents. Who knew?"

Considering they'd been acquainted for most of their lives through his younger sister, he wasn't sure if he felt slighted by that.

When was the last time he'd seen Marni? Had to have been the holidays last year. He studied her now. She looked different, more mature.

And she smelled good. Some kind of spicy, citrus scent that lingered in the air. Her cheeks had filled in. He remembered her face being much more angular. In fact, she'd filled in all over. Marni was definitely curvier than he remembered, bringing to mind images of starlets from the Hollywood of old. The likes of

Sofia Loren or Gina Lollobrigida. The changes looked good on her. *Marni* looked good.

And why in the world would he notice a thing like that? Gio gave himself a mental shake. Maybe his head injury wasn't as healed as he'd hoped. He had no business sniffing around his sister's best friend or waxing poetic about her curves. This was little *gattina*, for heaven's sake. "Little kitten." He couldn't even remember when he'd first given her the nickname. They'd been kids, and she'd reminded him of a kitten because she was always so playful and constantly underfoot.

She pointed to the kettle sitting by the side of the island. "Mind if I make some tea? If I know Nella, she's got some high-quality black leaf sitting around here somewhere."

He'd been about to suggest one of the bottles of high-end Chianti he'd discovered in the wine rack by the bar but tea would work. In fact, it might be better to keep sober around her given the wayward thoughts that kept popping in his head.

"Sounds good."

"I was thinking of getting ahold of Nella," she said, filling the silver kettle with water and setting it on the stove. "To ask her if there's a friend in town who might happen to have a room."

"Good idea," he answered. Better than anything he'd been able to come up with.

"As much as I hate to bother her and Alex on their romantic trip to Paris."

"They'll have to forgive us for the intrusion."

She nodded. "I would have done it already except I have no phone." She looked at him expectedly.

Gio popped a mozzarella ball into his mouth. "Yeah, it's really too bad that it shattered like that." He really did feel bad about scaring her so badly. He should find a way to apologize. Though it was hard to say sorry about something you weren't even aware was happening at the time.

"So…uh…could you maybe do it?" Marni asked.

Gio gave his head a shake. Of course! How daft could he be? What was wrong with him? Why couldn't he suddenly think straight around a woman he'd known practically his whole life?

Had to be the lack of sleep. It was wreaking havoc on his mental faculties. He pulled his phone out of his back pocket and clicked on his sister's name. Straight to voice mail. Not surprising. "No answer," he told Marni after leaving Nella a brief message he could only hope she would check in a timely fashion. "I'll try Alex next."

His brother-in-law's phone didn't even have the option to leave a voice mail. Gio just got the "unavailable" message. He shook his head at Marni's unvoiced question.

"Sorry. Can't reach him either."

Marni's face fell, her lips forming a thin line. She was really worried. A tinge of guilt tugged in his chest. She'd be kicking back and relaxing right now with a working phone if it wasn't for him. He couldn't seem to do anything right these days.

The dejected expression on her face tore at him. Gio had a crazy urge to go to her and gather her in his arms. Lucky for him, the kettle started screeching before he could do anything so foolish. Marni silently went to brew the tea, the look on her face not easing in the least.

"We'll figure this out," he reassured her. "In the meantime, it's not so bad being here with me, is it?"

But Marni only silently smiled in answer. Whatever she was hoping to get out of this trip, it was clear Gio's presence was going to be a hindrance. His guilt grew.

Within moments, Marni had found two ceramic mugs, had brewed the tea and had a steaming mug sitting in front of them both.

"We'll try Nella and Alex again in a bit."

"Something tells me they're not going to answer their phones anytime soon." Her voice was low and forlorn.

"Then we'll make do for now and start fresh tomorrow. And first thing in the morning, we'll head into town and see about replacing that phone."

If he'd thought that was going to cheer her up at all, he was sorely disappointed. Marni barely reacted to the offer. In fact, she appeared to be deep in thought, staring at the steam rising from her mug. For as excited as she'd seemed about the food, so far she'd barely taken a bite. Yep, Gio had inadvertently ruined Marni Payton's vacation.

Nothing he could do about it now. They just had to coexist for the next few hours until he could figure out a plan of action.

And as far as sleeping arrangements for the night, heaven only knew what they would do.

Marni lay awake staring into the darkness. It had all been too much to hope for. Was a two-week reprieve too much to ask for from the universe? All she'd wanted from this trip was to get away for a few days and lick her proverbial wounds. Just a chance to leave the past behind and focus on herself in quiet solitude in what she'd thought would be her friend's abandoned villa on the Italian coast. No such luck. Because enter one Gio Santino.

What was he doing here in Italy, anyway? He had a major corporation to run. Santino Foods was headquartered in the North End in Boston.

As CEO of Santino Foods, Gio rarely took time off. Even after a car accident last year, he'd barely given himself time away. Last she'd heard from Nella, he was putting off the therapy and the appointments recommended for a full recovery.

Regardless of his reason for being here, now Marni would have to find alternate arrangements. And she would have to be the one to leave. First of all, Gio had gotten here first. He was already settled while she hadn't even unpacked yet. Not to mention, his blood sibling actually owned the house. Marni and Nella had been friends for years—but blood trumped friendship.

Bad enough she'd kicked him out of the bed for the night. Gio had insisted. He'd told her he was having problems sleeping as it was. Now he was lying on a pile of cushions they'd taken off the couches downstairs and turned into a makeshift mattress on the floor of one of the empty rooms. Try as she might, Marni hadn't been able to convince him to take the real bed instead of her. Not surprising. She'd known the argument was futile from the beginning because Gio wasn't wired that way.

What a mess.

But none of this was her fault. She'd been planning this trip for weeks. Since the day she'd walked away from Ander for good, Marni knew she'd have to get far away from her ex. At least for the short term. Being anywhere near him right after the breakup was a recipe for disaster.

She could only imagine what Ander's thoughts on her current predicament might be. First, he'd tell her that he'd told her so. He'd remind her how little she was capable of without his guidance. That it was no wonder she'd messed up the very first thing she'd tried to do without him by her side.

Worst of all, Ander had plenty of contacts who were all too willing to print and air his version of events. It was why she'd had to get away, to find refuge in an entirely different country.

Marni sniffled away a tear and threw her forearm over her eyes. She refused to believe that Ander might be right about her. He liked to think she was useless and incompetent without him. That was just his narcissism. Being out from under his thumb and getting far away from him was the best thing Marni could have done for herself. Something she should have done much sooner.

As soon as she figured out her living situation for the next couple of weeks, everything would fall into place.

A loud shriek cut through the darkness. Marni bolted up in bed, disoriented and alarmed. She'd been closer to falling asleep than she thought. The loud noise sent her pulse rocketing.

Gio. Something was terribly wrong with him. Had someone broken in, after all? Was he struggling with an intruder right at this very moment?

Marni scrambled out of bed and ran to his room, grabbing a heavy vase off the bureau along the way. Her heart pounding, she threw open his door. Relief surged through her when she saw no one else was in there with him. But Gio was far from okay. A small sliver of moonlight from the open window illuminated just enough of the room to allow her to see him thrashing about on the cushions, his cries of anguish echoed off the walls. Whatever nightmare he was having seemed to be torturing him in his sleep. Marni rushed over to his side and dropped to her knees.

"Gio. Wake up," she cried. "You have to wake up."

Nothing. He hadn't even heard her. The thrashing didn't let up, his cries continued jarring the night air.

"Gio! It's me!" she yelled out, louder this time. She reached for his shoulders to give him a shake.

Big mistake. Gio didn't awaken but she'd managed to startle him in his sleep. His arms thrust out and he grabbed her by the arms, yanked her down. She landed on top of his chest, their legs intertwined.

Marni's vision went dark, her voice stuck in her throat. Scramble as she might, she couldn't get out of Gio's grip.

Panic and fear surged through her until she thought she'd completely lost her breath. Images rushed through her mind—all the times Ander had grabbed her arm just a little too roughly. The times he'd been frustrated with her when they were running late and given her a nudge just hard enough to be considered a push. The many moments she'd wondered if and when he'd go too far.

Steady. Ander wasn't here. This was Gio. And he would never hurt her. He was just having a nightmare.

The more she fought, the harder Gio held her. Marni forced herself to go still and take several deep breaths. It seemed to work. Gio's grasp loosened just enough for her to roll out of his reach.

Several moments passed while she tried to

regain a steady breath. Gio finally grew quiet, she was debating whether to simply stand and leave the room, when his eyes fluttered open. His gaze cast about the room, his dark brown eyes growing wide when they found her.

"Marni?"

She could only nod in response.

"What are you doing here?"

"I heard you…thought you might be hurt. Or someone might be here…" She couldn't seem to make her mind communicate with her mouth.

Gio's face tightened as he put the scenario together. Even in the dark, she could see the horror flood his features. He stood and rubbed a hand down his face. "Marni. I'm so sorry. I never meant to scare you. Again."

In two strides he'd reached the wall and flipped on the light switch. Soft yellow light flooded the room. Gio wore only pajama bottoms, hung low on his hips. Bare chested, she could see the hardened contours of his muscles.

So not the time to be noticing such a thing.

But she noticed something else. It was rather hard to miss. A large angry scar ran down the side of his torso down to his hip. It looked fresh and red.

Nella hadn't told her much about his accident. Though, truth be told, Marni had been too preoccupied with the emotional toll of her relationship with Ander to really pay attention. But judging by Gio's physical scars, the accident had been more serious than Marni had known.

No wonder Gio was having nightmares.

CHAPTER TWO

GIO WASN'T IN the house when she awoke the next morning. Marni had to wonder if he'd even managed to get back to sleep or if he even wanted to, given what awaited him in dreamland.

When he'd mentioned yesterday that he had trouble sleeping, she'd had no idea how violent his slumber could get. It certainly explained the squeaking she'd heard upon arrival at the house.

What exactly happened to him? The tabloids and gossip websites had moved past reporting on the story pretty quickly. The high-profile divorce of a Hollywood power couple had taken over the news feeds right around the same time. Nella didn't give away much either when Marni asked. There was a while a few months back where Nella looked particularly distracted. Worried, even. Marni hadn't wanted to pry at the time. She knew Gio and his sister were quite close. But she also knew both siblings could be withdrawn and very private.

She gave her head a brisk shake. It was too much to think about first thing in the morning after a restless night. She made her way to the kitchen for some much-needed caffeine.

A scrap of paper sitting on the counter caught her eye. Gio had left her a note.

Gone for a walk on the beach. Let's talk when I get back.

Fine by her. They had a lot to discuss. Like exactly what the plan was if neither of them could find another place to stay.

The sound of a standard ringtone shrilling behind her cut through her thoughts. Gio had left his phone behind. The sound reminded her that her own phone sat in the bottom of the rubbish bin in several pieces. She sighed with frustration. Yet another thing to deal with and fix.

Marni glanced at the screen. Nella! As if her thoughts from a few minutes ago had conjured her. Finally.

But Gio wasn't here. Marni raced to the small window above the sink to see if he was at all nearby. They both desperately needed to talk to his sister.

No sign of him.

Marni swore under her breath then rushed to pick up the call. Gio wouldn't mind if she answered his phone. Just this once. Not in this case. Before she could change her mind, she answered.

"Hey, Nella."

Several silent pauses followed. Marni could just picture the confusion on her friend's face about a thousand miles away as she tried to figure out what was what.

Nella sounded just as confused as she'd imagined when she finally spoke. "Marni? Is that you? I thought I dialed my brother."

"It is. I mean, you did."

Far from clearing anything up, Marni's response was a jumbled mess. She took a deep breath to try again. "Yeah, it's me. But you dialed right. This is your brother's phone. He's just out right now. So I didn't think he'd mind if I answered."

That wouldn't do much to clarify things either.

Nella spoke before she could try again at another lame attempt. "Marni, what's going on? Why are you answering my brother's phone? Where are you two and what are you doing together?"

Marni scrambled for the right words. Where exactly to begin? "Well, it's a funny story actually." Except it really wasn't.

"Tell me," Nella prodded.

"See, I decided to take you up on your offer to stay at your house in Capri for the next two weeks."

"Good," Nella said immediately. "You need it."

"Right. Well, I got here last night and, to my surprise—"

Nella cut her off before she could finish. "Let me guess, Gio was already there when you arrived."

"Bingo."

Marni heard a low whistle from the other end of the line. "He's had a key since we've owned the place, with a standing offer to use it as he wished when we aren't there. Though I can't recall the last time he's actually taken us up on it."

Just her typical lousy luck, then. "I see."

"I'm really sorry, Marni. I had no idea what he planned—he's supposed to be in Chicago."

"Chicago?" As far as she knew, Santino Foods had no presence in Illinois.

Nella cleared her throat. "Never mind, the point is I would have warned you if I had any clue that he might show."

"No need to apologize. This is your house. And he's your brother."

"And you're my dearest friend."

"It wasn't your mistake," Marni reassured.

"Still, I know how much you could use a get-away. And my brother is sort of hard to ignore."

That was an understatement. Gio was larger than life. Handsome, charming, with a sharp sense of humor. He'd always had a large personality.

Nella was still talking. "But I tried to call you last night. You didn't answer."

"Yeah, that's the other thing. I sort of destroyed my phone when I got to the villa. But that's a story for another day."

Marni cringed as the words left her mouth. Anyone but her best friend would probably deem her daft or clumsy. Or both. She'd arrived at an already occupied house and then promptly smashed her phone.

"Huh. I'd definitely like to hear it."

"Right. Well, now we're figuring out where I might move out to. If you have any suggestions."

"Move out? Why would you move out? The villa is huge."

When she put it that way, Marni was hard-pressed to come up with an answer. But she just couldn't imagine herself staying here when Gio was close by. Plus, there was the whole matter of the accommodations. "For one thing, there's only one bed."

"That's easy. Signora Baraca's son owns a furniture shop in town. Every piece is hand-crafted. We've been meaning to get those empty rooms furnished and never got around to it. I'll give her a call and you guys can go down and pick something."

Marni rubbed her forehead. "Nella, you should be the one decorating your house. Not me."

Nella laughed. Marni could almost see her waving her hand dismissively. "Why not? It's literally what you do for a living."

True, Marni was an interior decorator. But she usually did commercial work with plenty of input from whomever she was working for.

"I think you know me well enough to pick out pieces I'll like," Nella pressed.

Still. "I don't think Gio will agree, Nella." What if Gio needed time to himself? To deal with whatever he was trying to deal with. She had an urge to ask Nella more about the accident and Gio's scars but decided against it. Her friend would have told her before now if Marni was meant to know.

"Well, then that would be *his* problem, wouldn't it?" Nella answered. "And he'd have to be the one to find another place. He'll come around," she added after a pause. "He's not that stubborn."

"If you say so," Marni answered, not quite convinced. She'd seen Gio act plenty stubborn over the years.

"I do say so. Trust me. And, Marni?"

"Yes?"

"Please have my brother call me as soon as he gets in. I'd really like to talk to him." Was it her imagination, or did Nella sound slightly amused?

She was pondering that question several moments later when a loud sound jarred her in her seat. She took a deep breath. It was just the front door. Just Gio returning.

Honestly, she had to stop being so jumpy. She was in Capri now. Not back home in Massachusetts where there was someone constantly hovering over her shoulder, ready to hurl an insult or some type of accusation. Someone she'd thought she'd loved once.

When she'd been naive and too trusting. Never again.

"Marni?" Gio called from the doorway.

"In the kitchen."

When Gio entered the room, he brought with him the scent of fresh pastries. He held out a white cardboard box tied with a thin string. "I thought you might want some breakfast."

"Oh. Wow. Thanks."

Without another word, he set the box in front

of her. Huh. The gesture was so unexpected, Marni wasn't sure what else to say. She couldn't recall the last time someone had brought her breakfast. Or brought her anything, for no reason other than that she might enjoy it.

Ander would have never treated her to pastries. He considered such indulgences out of the question. Well, she didn't need to give his opinion another thought anymore. He would no longer be monitoring her calorie intake or anything else that concerned her. Never again.

She untied the string and lifted the cover to reveal an array of mouthwatering pastries that looked as delicious as they smelled. Croissants, bagels, a baguette, fruit-topped Danish with rich glaze. There had to be thousands of calories in this box.

But she didn't need to focus on that these days. Not unless she chose to do so. Ander didn't have the right to comment on her looks anymore or check whether she'd logged a calorie deficit or gain for the day.

"Where did you get these?" she asked, just for something to say and to pull herself out of the unwelcome thoughts.

"There's a stand on the beach. You should check it out. They have desserts in the evenings."

Marni sighed. Baked goods on the beach.

Exactly the kind of thing she'd been looking forward to when coming here. Could Nella be right? Could she and Gio just stay here? Together but apart? It would solve everything. Neither one would have to worry about finding another place. The only thing they'd need to do was find a bed and some furniture.

The villa was indeed a good size.

But would Gio see it that way? He was clearly here to get away from something, much like herself. What if the last thing he wanted was his little sister's pesky best friend underfoot?

Only one way to find out.

"So, your sister called," she told him. "You just missed her."

"Oh? About time."

Marni nodded. "She wants you to call her back. As soon as possible."

Gio shook his head, reached for a glass from the cabinet and poured himself water from the sink. "She's always so bossy," he complained, but his voice held no sting. Still. He wasn't in a rush to do as Nella had asked.

"I hope you don't mind, but I answered your phone when I saw on the screen that it was her calling."

He shrugged. "I guess that's okay. As long as she's the only one you answer my phone for."

That was weird. Why would she answer it

otherwise? But it was apparently important for him to set that boundary. Marni tipped three fingers to her forehead in a mock salute. "Aye, aye."

His privacy was clearly important to him, not surprisingly. Which probably didn't bode well for him agreeing to share the villa with her.

"Bet she was surprised to hear that we're both here."

"She certainly was."

"What did she have to say about it?"

Marni pursed her lips and pointed to his phone on the counter behind him. "I think you'd better call her now. Hear it all for yourself."

Well, that sounded pretty ominous. What had Nella and Marni discussed exactly? Though he'd been delaying returning Nella's call out of pure sibling pettiness—wanting him to get back to her ASAP when she'd taken her sweet time to return his call. As if.

But now his curiosity was piqued. Reaching behind him for his phone, he called up his sister's contact and dialed. When he looked up, Marni was no longer at the counter. The woman could move like a feline, as befitting his nickname for her. He hadn't even heard her leave.

His sister answered on the third ring. With

a string of curse words followed by some very specific thoughts about his intelligence and stubbornness.

"Good morning to you too, sis."

"Don't give me that," she snapped back. "What the devil are you doing in Capri? Of all places."

"Sorry. I thought you said I could use this place whenever I wanted."

Nella sighed loudly into the phone. "You know that's not what I mean. Of course any home I have is open to you at any time."

"Huh. You could have fooled me the way you answered my call."

Another Italian curse reached his ear. "Stop playing games, Gio. This isn't the time." Silence followed. A pause during which Nella's aggravation with him had been replaced by sisterly concern. "How are you, by the way?"

Gio was torn between irritation and affection. He was beginning to resent that question. It was all he'd heard for the past several weeks. From Mama, his sister, everyone who knew all the details about what had happened.

"I'm fine."

"Gio, you're not fine. You're supposed to be in Chicago seeing that orthopedic specialist and beginning rehab. Why in the world did you cancel?"

"I canceled because I'm feeling better." Not quite the truth, just a small fib. Gio pinched the bridge of his nose. Who was he kidding? It was a whopper of a lie and he deserved to be hit by a lightning bolt where he stood.

"I'm fine, Nella," he repeated. She may be his sister, but this was really none of her concern. "I just need another place to stay. Do you have any ideas? A neighbor who's away for the season? A hotel you'd recommend? I guess I could go to Naples, stay there..."

Nella sighed with clear resignation. "You don't need to go to Naples. You and Marni can both stay."

"There's only one bed."

"*Nessun problema.* I've already called the furniture store in town, told them to expect you."

Gio supposed that made sense. If Marni was okay with this arrangement, he could make it work.

Nella continued, "Having said that, dear brother, there's just one more thing."

With Nella there always was. "What's that?"

"Marni happens to be my oldest and dearest friend. She's like a sister to me."

"I know all that."

"So I trust you'll know not to toy with her."

Toy with her? She really wasn't going *there*,

was she? "Nella, what in the world are you getting at?"

"Let's not pretend you don't have a reputation as a ladies' man, Gio. Marni's too important."

"You've made your point, Nella."

"Please remember it."

Gio said goodbye and ended the call, trying not to feel offended. Did Nella really think she had to warn him off Marni? Of course he'd be mindful not to cross any boundaries with her. He'd known her too long, considered her part of their family.

Given his current situation, Gio was in no position to pursue anything romantic with anyone. Let alone the dear friend who Mama and his sister loved. He'd have the two of them to answer to when things went bad, as they inevitably would. He wasn't built for long-term relationships, especially not now. And Marni deserved more than a meaningless fling.

No, the bigger issue when it came to Marni, if they were going to stay here together for the next several days, was how long he could avoid questions about what was wrong with him.

"Nella thinks we should both stay put here," Gio announced as he walked out onto the patio several minutes later.

Marni looked up from the Italy travel site

she'd been perusing on her tablet. Not that she'd been able to pay attention to the colorful pictures of the many tourist attractions. She was much too preoccupied with the way Gio and Nella's phone call might have gone.

"She says the villa is spacious enough for the both of us," he continued. "And that all we need is to furnish one of the rooms."

Huh. Well, he wasn't laughing or grimacing, for that matter. It sounded like he was actually considering it.

"And what do you think?"

He pulled out the lounge chair next to her and plopped down. "It's your decision, *gattina*. I'm the one who came here unannounced."

"True. Which was very inconvenient of you by the way."

"As Nella made sure to let me know."

"But this happens to be your sister's house. And you have an open invitation to be here, unannounced or not."

Not to mention, he was clearly dealing with trauma horrible enough to have scarred his body and give him violent nightmares. A trauma he didn't seem in any kind of hurry to talk about.

"All right, *gattina*. I guess we've established that we both have a right to be here, then."

"I agree."

"Then I say we go furniture shopping," he declared, then grunted out a laugh. "Now, there's a line I never thought I'd say to a woman. And certainly not to my sister's best friend."

Marni bit down on the disappointment that washed through her at his words. His sister's friend. Little *gattina*. Gio had quite the reputation as a ladies' man. He had since he'd barely been a teenager. But he'd never see her as anything more than an extension of his sibling. A little playful kitten. Why that bothered her at this precise moment, she couldn't decide.

One theory that made sense was that her previous relationship had completely destroyed her self-esteem and confidence. So much so that she was now looking for validation from a man she should never view as anything more than a friend. And friends could be roommates. Especially if it was only a temporary arrangement.

Shutting her tablet, she rose out of her chair. "I'm ready when you are."

An hour later, Marni followed Gio out the door. But he surprised her when instead of heading toward the road, he turned toward the beach.

"Where are we going?" she asked his back, following him anyway.

"To town, remember?"

"But the road is behind us."

He turned to give her a curious glance. "But the ocean is in front of us. As is the boat."

"Boat?"

He finally turned to face her. "That's right. You know, it's a mode of transportation that's particularly useful on the water. Has these large white things called sails. And a motor."

Marni gave him a useless shove on his upper arm. He barely moved in response. "Ha ha. I know what a boat is. I just didn't realize we had one at our disposal."

"We do. And it's just as easy to sail up the coast as to try to get a taxi or catch the bus. You don't mind the water, do you, Marni?"

"I'm on an island, aren't I?"

He chuckled then turned back to the stone steps leading toward the water and continued down. Marni silently followed. They walked the beach about a quarter mile until they reached a small wooden pathway leading to the ocean. Half a dozen boats floated anchored at the end. Of course, Gio headed straight for the sleekest, newest-looking one.

"So I lied about the sails," he told her as he helped her aboard. "It's a motorboat."

The amount that Marni knew about boats could fit into a thimble. She could count on one hand all the times she'd been on one. Including the dinner cruise she'd taken with Ander last summer where he'd complained the entire time about the quality of the food and speed of service. Also, about her outfit. She remembered he'd chastised her about showing too much leg with that particular one. If she'd worn a tea-length gown, he would have found something else to complain about.

But that was nothing unusual.

Marni shook away the thoughts and allowed Gio to help her onboard. He walked over to a built-in bin and lifted the cover, removing two life jackets. He handed the smaller one to her. "Do you know how to put one of these on?"

Well, she wasn't that clueless about sailing. "Yes. But is it absolutely necess—"

He didn't even let her finish the sentence. "Yes. We don't even lift anchor unless you have it on nice and tight. Otherwise, you can just turn around and get off right now."

Marni swallowed. Everything about Gio's demeanor had just changed. As soon as she'd begun to ask the question, his eyes flashed dark and the muscles around his mouth tightened.

She hardly recognized this side of him. The Gio she knew would have made light of her resistance, made some kind of quip about not diving in to rescue her if she were to end up in the water. Gio's expression now held no mirth whatsoever.

"Harsh," she muttered, yanking the preserver out of his hands. Without another word, she put it on then clipped the holster clasps shut. Gio studied her the entire time, as if not fully trusting her to do it properly. She glared at him, lifting her arms. "Do you care to inspect it?"

The corner of his mouth lifted ever so slightly as his eyes traveled down her body.

"As tempting as that is, I've been warned against such inappropriate behavior." With that he turned to stride toward the dashboard, throwing his own life jacket on in the process.

Marni felt hot color flush her cheeks. A tingling awareness skittered over her skin.

He'd been warned? What in heaven's name did that mean?

CHAPTER THREE

Gio turned the steering wheel and began to guide the boat toward the town marina. A bright orange sun hung in a crystal blue sky, and the waves shimmered like liquid gems as they moved along the surface of the water.

If someone had told him a week ago that he'd be spending the day furniture shopping with Marni Payton, he would have told said person to check their mental state. Yet, as ridiculous as it was, he was about to go pick out bedding and floor rugs with little gattina, the same girl who'd followed him around like a pest with his sister for a good chunk of his years growing up.

But she looked very different than that little girl right now. In fact, there was nothing girlish about her. The lanky teen she'd once been had grown into a strikingly attractive young woman. He'd tried hard not to notice those changes over the years. It was harder to do so now in such proximity.

Maybe this living-together thing wasn't such a great idea, after all.

He studied her from the corner of his eye while she sat stern side, her gaze studying the distant horizon. Long, chestnut brown hair secured in a tight ponytail. So tight it seemed to be pulling at the skin around her face. A collared sleeveless shirt atop pressed capri pants. Sensible leather flat-heeled shoes adorned her feet. She looked like she could be going into the office for a day full of meetings.

Did the woman even know she was on vacation?

He would have to make sure she realized it at some point. Tell her to relax, loosen up a bit.

Not that it was any of his business. He had enough to deal with on his own plate.

Still, he couldn't help but wonder what had brought her out here. Alone. And she certainly didn't seem to be in vacation mode just yet. Rather than getting away, Marni looked to be running away from something.

His thoughts led him to remember the last time he'd seen her before this trip. She'd been thin to the point of looking gaunt, dark circles had framed her eyes, her lips continually thinned in a worried line. When he'd asked his sister if Marni was okay, Nella had alluded to a bad relationship. In fact, the look on his sister's face had turned downright murderous when she'd answered his question.

What kind of demons was Marni running from? Were they as bad as his?

Suddenly, he felt like a jerk for the way he'd reacted when she'd scoffed about putting on the life jacket. He could have been gentler. But he wasn't going to risk her well-being in any way. He of all people knew how a split-second moment of carelessness could result in a monumental catastrophe with a lifetime of dire consequences.

Not on his watch. Not this time.

A chuckle rose out of him when he recalled how she'd reacted, challenging him to inspect the life jacket. How tempted he'd been to do just that. To run his fingers down her throat with the pretense of checking the clasps' tightness. To tug her tight ponytail out from beneath the vest, then run his hands through the thick, curly waves.

Whoa. Gio gave his head a shake.

"What is it?" Marni asked.

"Huh?"

She smiled at him. "You were just laughing at something," she said. "Can I get in on the joke?"

He certainly couldn't tell her where his mind had really been.

You see, Marni, I was thinking about the way

*your skin might feel under my fingertips, how
the strands of your hair might flow over my
hands, the way you smell of lemon and rose and
some combination of spice I can't quite name.*

No, definitely wouldn't go over well. Gio
scrambled for a response. But it was hard to
think with the way Marni was smiling at him
as the sunlight danced along her eyes and glim-
mered in her hair.

What was wrong with him?

No matter. He just had to stop. Best way
would be reverting to his go-to behavior when
it came to Marni. Teasing her like an older
cousin might.

"If you must know," he began, "I was thinking how you look like you're about to go to a
board meeting as opposed to spending a care-
free day on a Mediterranean island in one of
the most gorgeous countries on earth."

Her mouth fell open. "What's that supposed
to mean?"

He shrugged, and turned his gaze back to
the water. "Start with your shoes for example."

She lifted one elegant leg and looked at her
foot. "What's wrong with my shoes?"

"I think Nonno Santino owned a pair just
like that, but in taupe."

She dropped her chin to her chest, glaring
at him. Okay, maybe he was being a bit over-

the-top. In truth, his *nonno* had worn nothing but tennis shoes.

"I'll have you know, these are quite comfortable," Marni protested.

"Is that why you shook sand out of them twice already?"

"I didn't know we'd be walking along the beach, now did I?" Her voice rose just enough to convey annoyance and irritation while remaining steady. "You could have mentioned we'd be taking a boat into town before we'd left the villa."

He nodded. "I could have. And you could have dressed less like a librarian about to begin a full shift."

Marni crossed her arms in front of her chest. "Yeah? What about the way you're dressed?" She gestured toward him with a fling of her hand.

Gio looked down at his wrinkled T-shirt, hip-hugging sports shorts and loose leather sandals. "What about it?"

"We're about to enter one of the most elegant shopping centers in Europe and you're wearing what could best be described as 'frat boy who caught the wrong flight heading to spring break.'"

Gio couldn't help it, he threw his head back

and laughed at her put-down. "Touché, little gattina. Touché."

Good for her, she was giving it right back.

She'd felt safe returning Gio's barbs. Marni knew his insults weren't really meant to wound her. A world of difference existed between the way Ander's constant criticisms were delivered and Gio's good-natured joking. She was surprised she even remembered how to verbally defend herself. Leave it to Gio Santino to remind her.

Forget that she'd been totally disingenuous when teasing Gio about his appearance.

The truth was, he somehow managed to look handsome and polished despite his beyond casual attire. No one in their right mind would ever confuse Gio for an out-of-place college student. No, even dressed in a T-shirt and sandals, he looked every bit the successful tycoon and CEO of a global corporation that he was. Now, as they disembarked from the boat and made their way down the sidewalk path along the street of shops, it was clear she wasn't the only woman nearby who appreciated Gio's looks.

Tall, dark, with an angular jaw and toned, muscular body. His hair just long enough to reach his shoulders in dark waves…

Just stop.

This was not the time or place to be admiring Gio's looks or sex appeal. Heavens! Why had she even thought that last part?

Yanking her thoughts from such dangerous territory, Marni focused instead on her surroundings. Glamorous designer boutiques, mouthwatering bakery window displays, the tangy scent of citrus in the air as they passed a limoncello store. They were on a mission with a goal right now, but she made a mental note to come back into town soon and visit every one of these delightful places. Such a shame that she'd be doing so alone. The only reason Gio was here with her now was to pick out the bed one of them would be sleeping in. He'd have no incentive to play tour guide or tourist and return here with her afterward. Hadn't they agreed that the only way the cohabitation would work was to do their best to stay out of each other's way?

If that thought had her feeling downbeat and lonely, then it was no one's fault but her own. Gio wasn't her guardian. He didn't owe her anything, including his time.

Deep in thought, she nearly walked into Gio's solid back before realizing he'd stopped in front of the revolving glass door of a shop.

"This is it," he announced, then pulled the door open for her.

It was like walking into her own version of heaven. Beautiful works of art in the form of handcrafted wood furniture greeted them inside. It was hard to decide which item to study first: the beautiful bookshelf with the mahogany trim? Or the three-drawer bureau with the intricate carvings. Or maybe the standing mirror with the cherrywood base.

She was startled by a pair of snapping fingers right in her line of vision.

"Earth to Marni. You in there, Ms. Payton?"

She blinked to focus on Gio's face just inches from hers, expecting to find impatient annoyance in his impression. Instead, she found him smiling widely at her.

"Sorry, I was just admiring all the craftsmanship."

He dropped his hand, the grin still framing his lips. "I'll say. I've never seen such pleasure flood a woman's face so quickly. Not from just walking into a store, anyway." He winked at her mischievously.

Marni's mouth went dry at the innuendo. Before she could recover enough to formulate an answer, Gio had turned on his heel and walked farther into the store.

If she didn't know any better, she would think

Gio Santino might be flirting with her. Which was preposterous. In all their years of knowing one another, not once had Gio even hinted at any kind of attraction toward her, while she'd harbored a crush on and off for as long as she could remember. It didn't mean anything. Gio couldn't help himself. It was simply his nature to be charming and flirtatious. She just happened to be the only one in his vicinity at the moment. Giving her head a shake, she forced her focus back on the matter at hand: the furniture. They were here to pick something out of this gallery of masterpieces. Something told her she was going to be absolutely torn when it came to settling on just one item.

Despite her professionally trained eye, she felt like the kid in a candy store who wanted to grab everything and run home with her stash. She took her time making her way to where Gio stood, delicately trailing her fingers along the finished lines of the pieces in her path. When she reached his side, he pointed to a bed frame to his left. "What about that one?" he asked.

"What about it?"

He turned to squint at her. "Should we get that one?" he asked, as if his question should have been obvious.

Marni could only shake her head and laugh. He was approaching this outing as if they were replacing the milk carton in the fridge. Poor soul, he had no idea that they'd be in here for at least an hour, more likely much longer than that while she put a room together that would feel both cozy and pleasing to the eye of whoever inhabited it.

She shook her head at him. "Gio. You don't just come into a place like this and point."

His eyes narrowed on her face. "Why ever not? How else would we pick something?"

"We don't just pick something."

More narrowing of the eyes. "We don't?"

"No. We think about what we want the room to feel like for the inhabitant."

He crossed his arms in front of his chest. "Huh. I'd say it should feel like there's a sturdy piece of furniture in there to be able to sleep on after the day is over."

Of course, he would simplify it that way. "Okay. But beyond that, what do we want to feel when we enter that room? Warmth? Comfort? A sense of solitude?"

Gio rubbed his chin. "I'd say all of the above."

Marni threw her hands in the air. This was hopeless. She turned to walk further toward the back of the store. Gio followed close on her heels. After several moments of browsing, she could practically feel the impatience resonating off Gio's body.

"Fine," she heard him say behind her. "What about this one?"

He had to be kidding. He was pointing to a small child's bed designed to look like a pirate ship. "You can't be serious. You wouldn't even fit in that."

"When did we decide that I'd be the one to have to take the new room?"

Huh. He had a point. She hadn't actually considered that.

"Look," Gio continued. "At this point, I'd settle for a cot and a throw pillow. We've been in here for how many hours already?"

Marni made a show of lifting her wrist and staring at her watch. "We've been in here fifteen minutes."

Gio rubbed his forehead. "Huh. I was exaggerating but it feels longer than just a few minutes."

Marni sighed. As much as she wanted to linger in here, Gio had clearly reached the end of his patience. "Fine. I think your pirate ship just might have given me an idea."

Gio smiled wide, clearly pleased with himself. "Oh, yeah? How so?"

She gave him the "follow me" sign with her finger. "Here, I'll show you." The bed frame she led him to had tall posts above the headboard, and then she pointed out a round-framed mirror that could easily be accented to look like a porthole window. Rather than bedside tables for the lamps, she picked out two wooden coffers that, with the right studding, could be made to look like treasure chests.

"What do you think?" she asked Gio, after they'd gotten a chance to look at all the pieces.

"Huh. It will be like the bottom of an old-fashioned ship."

She smiled at him. "Maybe even like a pirate ship."

Gio tilted his head, examining her. "I like it, gattina. Well done!"

Marni felt a fluttering in her chest at his approval. It made no sense. She'd simply done what she was trained to do. So how utterly silly of her to feel so giddy at having pleased him.

Unlike the sparse compliments her ex threw her way from time to time, Gio's appreciation of her talent sounded genuine.

She'd almost forgotten what that felt like.

Gio signed the paperwork for the sale of the pieces Marni had picked out and led her out of the store twenty minutes later. For all the complaining he'd done in there, he had to begrudgingly admit that he'd actually enjoyed himself. Observing the way Marni's mind worked out a theme and put together a design had been more entertaining than he would have guessed. Watching her work had exposed him to a side of her he hadn't witnessed or even thought about before. She was smart, talented and had a clear enthusiasm for her chosen field.

Envy blossomed in his chest. He was a man of wealth and vast resources, but despite all his professional success, he couldn't recall the last time he'd felt accomplished and fulfilled.

Most times, he simply felt empty. Directionless.

Maybe that was why he took so many risks with his life, both physically and financially. Simply to *feel* something on any scale. It was that recklessness that had led him to fast cars and racing. Look how that had turned up. He'd damaged his body and hurt an innocent bystander to boot.

"Where to now?" Marni asked, pulling him out of the black hole of his thoughts.

In perfect timing, his stomach answered with a short growl. Marni's chuckle in response had him laughing as well. "How about we grab a bite?"

She pointed to his midsection. "I don't dare argue after that."

Within minutes they were seated at an outside table of Pescare Delfino seafood restaurant. Later afternoon had turned the sky a bluish gray. Two servers in black bow ties and buttoned vests appeared at their table before they'd so much as pulled in their chairs. One lit a large round candle in the centerpiece while the other poured limoncello in two small shot glasses.

Gio ordered a bottle of his favorite Pinot Grigio then held up his glass of limoncello once both waiters had left. "A toast."

Marni lifted her drink and clinked it to his. "What are we toasting to?" she asked.

"We are now officially roommates. For one."

They both took a sip of the refreshing liqueur, though Marni's could be described as more of a drop. Probably smart. The limoncello in Italy could be potent.

"What else?" Marni asked.

"To your stellar skills as an interior decorator. I'm sure you'll reach the highest pinnacles of success with your talent."

Something flashed behind her eyes, a darkness that shadowed the light that had been behind them since they'd first entered the furniture store.

"Um…thanks," she murmured, setting her glass down without another drink. She looked off into the distance.

Was it something he said? Gio had only meant to pay her a compliment.

Gio went the feigned ignorance route. "Do you not like the limoncello?" he asked, knowing full well that disappointment in her drink wasn't what had dimmed the brightness in her eyes from just moments before.

She immediately shook her head. "No. It's delicious. I guess I'm just hungry."

Sure. That wasn't the issue either. Talking about her professional success had completely soured her mood. Did her career have anything to do with why she was here in Capri for the next several days? Maybe a job she'd done had gone wrong and her ego had taken a hit.

Well, he wasn't one to push. Marni clearly didn't want to talk about her job. That was fine since he definitely didn't want to talk about his accident.

And if he ignored the pain and fought hard enough to continue hiding the limp, he wouldn't have to.

Marni searched for a change of topic. She wasn't in the mood to discuss the train wreck that was her current professional situation. If Ander Stolis had his way, she'd be persona non grata in all the circles that mattered as far as the interior design profession was concerned. And he'd make sure that would be the case for the foreseeable future.

Served her right for falling for the lead architect of the firm she'd worked for. At first, Marni had thought their budding relationship was so romantic. An office romance. Exciting and slightly taboo. Just like in all those romcoms. Little had she known, she'd be living more of a drama-tragedy.

"Do you know what you're having?" Gio asked across the table, breaking into her thoughts.

"A good heap of regret with a side of crow," she answered, then immediately clasped a hand to her mouth. What in the world was wrong with her? She hadn't meant to say the words out loud. The limoncello couldn't be that strong, for heaven's sake. She'd barely had one sip!

Gio reached out his arm across the table and covered her free hand with his.

"Hey, is everything all right with you?"

He asked so gently, with such care and interest, that Marni felt a lump of emotion form in her throat. She forced a smile on her lips. "I'm fine. Really."

He looked less than convinced and gave her wrist a small squeeze. His palm and fingers felt strong and warm over her hand. The eyes looking into hers held a wealth of concern. "You know you can tell me, gattina. If you want to."

Marni closed her eyes and blew out a deep breath. Gio didn't need to hear how stupid and blind she'd been. How she'd ignored all the warning signs as well as the good advice of her friends and family. The way she'd been certain she knew better than all the people who were only trying to protect her.

But it was so tempting to get some of it off her chest for once. "I made some bad decisions over this past year," she finally managed to answer. "Countless errors of judgment that caught up to me. The gist of it is that I trusted the wrong man."

Gio merely nodded, no judgment clouded his eyes, no subtle admonishment. That made it a bit easier for her to continue.

"I took longer than I should have to break things off with him. When I did, he used his considerable influence and high-profile contacts to smear my name and professional reputation."

She didn't miss the clench of Gio's fists on the table. "I see."

Swallowing, she continued. "He's a highly respected architect with several clients who are members of the media. I know it wouldn't be above him to sully my name in the professional magazines and websites. That's the last thing I need at this point in my career."

"That's why you're here."

She nodded. "That's right. Not only to get

away from it all until people lose interest. But also to try and regroup. Figure out how to climb out from under the mountain of mistakes and all their consequences."

Gio swore. "I'm sorry, Marni. If it makes you feel any better, you don't have the corner on bad decisions." He gestured to his chest with his thumb. "Your new roomie here has made a few doozies himself."

Profound hurt resonated in his voice. Gio clearly had his own mountain to climb. Perhaps he would understand her predicament better than most.

Marni turned her hand over under his, reflexively intertwining her fingers with his so that they were holding hands atop the table. She didn't let go until the server arrived to take their order.

CHAPTER FOUR

A SURGE OF protectiveness so strong rushed through Gio that he had to will himself to clamp it down. Marni was gripping his hand as if starved for strength and comfort.

What a lousy stroke of luck for her. He hardly had either of those for himself. He should let go of her, pull his arm back by his side. Find a way to lighten this conversation that had suddenly grown so heavy and deep.

He wanted badly to ask more about the man who'd caused her such deep hurt. But it was her prerogative to share as much or as little as she was ready to. Still, the curiosity didn't settle well in his gut. It was no use trying to tell himself it was none of his business. This was Marni. She'd practically grown up with the Santinos as part of the family. She was the only child of a single mother, and Gio knew how much she'd endured to simply survive her younger years.

They'd met her when her mom worked briefly for Santino Foods decades ago.

Despite Marni's disadvantages, she'd grown up to be a successful, confident woman with a list of accomplishments. He didn't know the details but someone had come along and ruined all that for her.

If he ever found out who it was and what exactly he'd done to her…

The waiter arrived with his scratch pad to take their order. They both pulled their hands away at the same moment; a rather awkward moment tempered only by the presence of their server.

When their salads arrived a few minutes later, that awkwardness still hung in the air. Finally, Marni was the one who broke the silence.

"You mentioned your own mistakes," she began, poking at the vegetables on her plate rather than eating any of them. "Do those mistakes have anything to do with your sleepless nights?"

Gio swallowed the plum tomato he'd been chewing, though not tasting. His mind juggled a confusion of thoughts. He didn't know how to talk about the accident and, so far, he hadn't wanted to with anyone. It was bad enough having to go through the details with every doctor and nurse who'd had to evaluate him in the days since. And he couldn't even quite remember all the details.

Where would he even begin to try and tell Marni? The reckless decision to race the car in the first place? How lucky he was that his passenger hadn't been killed? That the man may never walk again thanks to Gio?

Or maybe he could begin with how he might never have full use of his leg, no matter how many long hours of rehab he was made to endure. The dull ache in his thigh muscle mocked his train of thought. Marni picked up on his hesitation.

"You don't have to tell me," she said. "But know that you can," she added. "Same goes for you, because I'm little gattina, remember? Your sister's old friend."

Gio forced a smile he didn't feel. The trouble was, he was starting to view Marni as less and less of his little sister's old friend with each passing moment.

Such a dangerous development. Because the way he *was* beginning to view her spelled nothing but trouble for them both.

On the boat ride back to the villa, the early evening sky had turned navy, full of twinkling bright stars. The day had gone by in the blink of an eye. As tired as she was, Marni didn't quite want it to end. The hours she'd spent in town with Gio had been the most relaxed she'd been since her "walk of shame" through the office hallway. A shudder racked her body at the memory.

"You cold?" Gio asked, mistaking her shiver for physical discomfort.

He took her silence as a positive answer. Lifting open a center console, he removed a thick, zippered hoodie bearing the logo of the Los Angeles Angels across its back. He draped it over her shoulders, giving them a squeeze for good measure. Though it should have felt bulky and uncomfortable over the life jacket, Marni found herself snuggling into the soft fabric. It smelled of him: spicy, woodsy and oh so masculine. She buried her face in the collar, inhaling as she did so.

Suddenly horrified that Gio might have witnessed the small action, she yanked the fabric off her face. A glance in his direction told her he hadn't seen. He was focused on guiding the boat back to their destination. Marni breathed a sigh of relief. That was much too close. She'd be beyond embarrassed if Gio had any hint of her reemerging girlish crush.

It couldn't happen. Her emotions were already strung tight. She had no business crushing on a man so far beyond her reach. Sure, he was easy to talk to and they had a history of being friends. She felt lighter after having confided in him as much as she had about her fiasco of a relationship.

But their differences were plenty. Gio was several years older, and had been linked to women like starlets and models and heiresses. She knew better than to pine for someone like him. She'd just turned twenty-six last month for Pete's sake. She was too old for a schoolgirl crush. How had she not grown out of it already? Then there were the close familial ties. She wouldn't be able to bear it if there was tension between her and the Santino clan for any reason whatsoever.

No, better to just ignore her feelings and hope they went away.

It was just her mind trying to distract her. It had to be. Her brain was trying to stall figuring out all the things she had to deal with as soon as she got back to reality. Like how she might begin to restore her professional reputation. Whether she wanted to remain in Boston or relocate so she could put the past year behind her and move forward with her life.

Then there was the dream of starting her own design business. If she had the wherewithal or the resources or even the motivation to attempt such an undertaking. Another failure might completely undo her.

She was so deep in her thoughts, she hadn't even realized Gio had docked the boat and dropped anchor.

"You're not falling asleep on me, are you?" he asked.

"Guess that dinner was more filling than I thought, not to mention the strong cocktail. I do feel pretty lethargic."

"Then you're in luck," he told her while he finished securing the boat. "Because I happen to make a mean cappuccino. Not too strong, with plenty of frothy milk. It'll perk you right up without keeping you up all night."

Maybe it was wishful thinking, but it sounded as if Gio didn't quite want the night to end either.

"Sounds great." She decided to broach the subject they still hadn't gotten around to solving until the new furniture arrived. "I think you should sleep in the room tonight," she began as they made their way up the stone steps. "I'll be perfectly fine on the couch cushions."

Gio immediately shook his head. "Absolutely not. The bed is all yours."

She wasn't the least bit surprised that he'd immediately refused the offer. "It's only fair," she tried to argue. "I had it last night."

Gio didn't answer until they reached the top of the cliffside. He took her by the shoulders and turned her to him. "Marni. I'm not even sleeping for any stretch of time. Wasting the bed on me doesn't make sense."

Marni knew any further argument would be useless. With a sigh of resignation, she followed him down the path that led to Nella's villa. When they got to the house, Gio fired up the espresso machine while she indulged in a hot shower. He had a steaming mug waiting for her when she emerged a little while later.

"Want to enjoy these outside by the pool?"

That sounded like a delightful idea. Nella's outdoor lounge chairs were so plush and comfortable. And the night was warm with a soft, gentle breeze. Marni couldn't think of a single reason to turn down his offer.

"Lead the way," she answered, taking her cappuccino in hand.

Marni winced when they reached the patio and she eyed her tablet still sitting on the cushion. She'd forgotten her device out here when they'd left earlier. "Darn it."

"What's the matter?"

"I meant to charge that. Hopefully there's enough battery left."

"For what?" Gio asked, dropping onto one of the other chaise lounges.

She ducked shyly. "Don't laugh. But there's a Bollywood show I'm addicted to. I downloaded the latest episode and was looking forward to watching it later tonight."

"A bolly what now?"

She had to laugh at his confusion. "Bollywood. Filmed in India. The script is full of drama and intrigue with lots of song and dance thrown in for good measure."

"How do you understand it?"

She shrugged. "Captions, of course. It's like reading and enjoying an engrossing movie at the same time. You should try it."

Gio gave her a skeptical look. "I don't know. It doesn't really sound like my genre of entertainment."

Marni flipped the lid of her tablet and turned on the device. To her surprise and delight, she had a good amount of battery life left.

Pulling a chaise lounge next to him, she called up the show. "Here. Just try a few minutes. You might be surprised."

He tilted his head. "Sure. Why not. What else have I got to do?" he asked then scooched his chair closer while she touched the play icon. "Just don't tell my sister, or anyone else for that matter, that you talked me into watching a foreign film with captions."

Marni pressed her fingers to her mouth. "My lips are sealed. Our secret."

Gio shifted in the lounge chair and kicked out his legs to give them a good stretch. On instinct, he braced himself for the sharp pain that was sure to shoot down his thigh at any second. But the ache stayed dull and low. That was different. Usually, no matter how gentle the stretch, it always resulted in knifelike pain for several seconds.

In surprise, he blinked one eye open. Huh. The sun was out. But how could that be? The last thing he remembered, he and Marni were watching something on her tablet. A show it would normally never occur to him to watch. It had been close to midnight when the last thing he remembered—a funny dance number—had come on.

Which meant he must have fallen asleep right here. Outside on the lounge chair. More surprisingly, he'd apparently stayed asleep until sunrise…for several hours. A rarity that hadn't happened since the accident.

So that was a bit of stunning news that would take some processing.

It was when he tried to rise that he noticed an unfamiliar weight snuggled against his side. That could only mean one thing. Forcing both eyes open, Gio bit down on a groan at the sight that greeted him. He hadn't been the only one to fall asleep out here. Marni was snuggled against his length, her eyes closed shut in slumber.

Don't you dare react. Don't so much as move.

Not yet. He had no idea what he might say to Marni if she were to wake up right now. He was having trouble putting it all together himself. Besides, what would be the harm in letting her get some more rest? Something told him Marni had had her own share of restless nights recently.

He thought back to the dinner they'd shared the night before, the strain in her voice when she'd talked about her hurtful relationship, the way her lips had grown tight, her eyes clouded over with sadness. She'd trusted the wrong man. Hardly the first woman to do so. At least she hadn't made the kind of mistake that had almost cost someone else their life.

Sweet gattina, how hard are you punishing yourself anyway?

A seagull soared overhead, suddenly dropping to land on the patio by their feet. The noise was enough to have Marni stirring in his arms. Maybe he was being cowardly, but Gio immediately shut his eyes and feigned sleep. Why not spare them both some awkward embarrassment if it could be helped?

He sensed the moment she must have opened her eyes and discovered their positions. He felt her whole body go tense, a small gasp sounded beneath his ear. It took all his will not to open his eyes out of sheer curiosity. It might be worth it to see the expression on her face.

Gio felt her move softly out of his arms and scramble off the chair. The seagull squawked above and he almost reflexively opened his eyes in response. But somehow managed to continue the pretense until he heard the screen door leading to the house open before it softly shut closed again.

He gave her a good twenty minutes before finally following her inside. Marni stood at the counter of the kitchen, brewing tea. She'd changed into a pair of loose gray sweats and a tunic-length shirt that fell low off one shoulder to reveal a small triangle of smooth skin. His nerve endings tingled as he recalled how that skin had felt in his arms moments ago.

How the woman managed to look so sexy in sweats and a loose T-shirt, with her hair a tangled mess, Gio couldn't explain. Her eyes grew wide when she saw him.

"Morning," Gio said before she could speak. "Can you believe I fell asleep outside?" He shook his head as if amused with himself. "I must have been so tired."

Marni nodded. "Actually, I—"

He pretended not to hear her as he made a show of stretching his arms overhead while executing a perfectly believable loud yawn. Maybe one day they would laugh about the way they'd fallen asleep in each other's arms. He just didn't have it in him to do it today. Not after the way he'd reacted to having her body so close to his. Something told him Marni wouldn't be up for such a conversation either. "Hard to believe, but it's the best night's sleep I've had in forever."

"Huh."

He dropped his arms. "Guess I'll go take a shower."

She blinked several times in rapid succession but didn't say anything. Bingo. He'd been right. Marni was just as content to ignore the fact that they'd fallen asleep in each other's arms as he was. What was the point in dwelling on it? It wasn't as if anything physical had happened between them, after all. No boundaries had been breached whatsoever. And thank God for that. He had enough to deal with right now without crossing any lines with his kid sister's best friend. Nella's warning echoed in his head. *If you do anything to hurt her or make her uncomfortable...*

He pointed to the kettle, which started steaming. "Can you spare some of that for me when I get back?"

Marni nodded. "Of course, I'll have a mug waiting for you."

"Thanks."

See, all casual. Nothing amiss. Just two old friends who happened to be sharing the same living space for a few days. Then they would both go their separate ways and this would just be one more memory of Marni Payton that he'd add to all the other ones.

No one had to know that the shower he'd be taking would be a cold one.

Gio stood under the steaming hot spray, relishing the soothing flow of water over his skin. After a punishing blast of it at ice cold to get his libido under control, he'd turned the nozzle completely the opposite way to the hottest setting.

Not that the cooler water had helped at all. His mind kept going back to that one exposed shoulder. The way the tunic shirt had draped her curves in all the right places.

The way she'd felt in his arms when he'd awakened to find her nuzzled against his side.

Gio swore and pushed the wayward thoughts away, then squeezed more of the soap onto his hand. He usually massaged his sore leg every morning in the shower, the one piece of medical advice he'd taken so far. But the bruised and tattered muscles still felt remarkably less sore.

Had he taken a pain pill and forgotten? No. He hadn't been that out of it. Besides, he did his best to avoid the pills unless he was in absolute agony. The more likely scenario was that he'd done less thrashing about with his legs because he'd subconsciously known that he'd disturb Marni. Or maybe one good night of sleep at last had done both his spirit and body a world of good. Somehow, falling asleep next to Marni while watching a fun, mindless show had given him that rare gift.

Gio sighed and braced his hands against the tile wall. Too bad it couldn't happen again.

Spending time with her was good for him, there was no denying. But there was no way he was going to take advantage of her for his own selfish needs.

The truth was, on his best day, he wouldn't have been worthy of Marni Payton. And these days he was far from his best. Not since the race that had changed him forever.

Before he could suppress them, an onslaught of visions flooded his brain. Losing control of the wheel, veering off at too high a speed toward the other car. The flash of light as the flames burst forth.

He knew he was lucky to be alive. But he felt a mere partial version of the man he used to be. Why would he subject any woman to what his future had waiting for him? Countless days in therapy. A permanent limp. The certain frustration and resulting poor temperament all that was sure to bring out in him.

No. Marni deserved better than that. She deserved better than *him*.

Why was he even traveling down this road of thought? He and Marni as any kind of item were out of the question. He had enough to figure out about his own life without the complication of a romantic relationship. Let alone with someone who meant as much to his family as Marni did.

Nella had warned him about not pursuing this very thing.

That was it. The shower was doing nothing to relax him at this point. Rather than soothing him in any way, now the steam felt oppressively hot and the stall felt suffocating. He pushed aside the glass door and grabbed the thick Turkish towel he'd hung up before his shower.

His phone sounded an alert in the other room. One he'd assigned to his assistant.

Might want to check your email, boss.

Gio did as her message said then cursed out loud. A reporter for New England magazine was asking questions about the accident again after all this time. The last thing Juno needed as he tried to recover was any kind of media attention. The man deserved his privacy as he healed. Gio had to find a way to shut this down as soon as possible.

He was about to text a reply when another message appeared on his screen. This one from his sister.

How are you today?

Honestly, she had to stop asking him that. He wasn't even going to bother to respond to the question. He asked one of his own instead.

Do you know when the new furniture might arrive?

The floating bubbles appeared on the screen once more.

No update yet.

Gio pinched the bridge of his nose and sighed. Nella was still typing.

But I just got word that there's a villa available to buy. If you're still interested in getting your own place in Capri.

CHAPTER FIVE

WELL, IF SHE'D harbored any illusions that Gio was in any way affected by her, she'd been proven sorely mistaken.

He hadn't even noticed her presence next to him last night. She might as well have been a teddy bear he'd been cuddling.

Whereas she couldn't stop thinking about the feeling of being in his arms, the warmth of his body surrounding hers. The scent of him filling her senses when she'd awakened with her head on his chest.

Now she couldn't seem to stop thinking about him upstairs in the shower. Surrounded by steam, water and soapy suds flowing down his hardened muscles.

Marni groaned out loud. This couldn't be happening. She couldn't be reviving her childhood crush, it was completely one-sided. It had to be. Gio may have seemed to be flirting with her sometimes, but that was just his nature, it was how he reacted with any woman in his vicinity.

How could she be lusting after a man who hadn't even realized he'd fallen asleep with her against his side?

Her breath hitched in her throat when she heard him shut the door upstairs and make his way down the stairs. If she was going to squelch this crush, she would have to start with not becoming breathless when she so much as heard the man. He entered the kitchen a moment later, looking fresh and clean, his hair damp. He smelled of pine and mint and his own distinctive masculine scent.

She greeted him with what she hoped was a convincingly friendly smile. "Just in time. Your tea was about to get cold."

"Would have come down sooner, but I was delayed."

"Oh?"

"Nella messaged. Says hello. She tried to call you but I guess you haven't set up your phone yet."

She'd meant to. But she'd been much too distracted last night and this morning. By him.

"I'll make sure to get ahold of her later."

"Sounds good." He took a sip of his tea. "So, how'd you sleep?"

Was it her imagination, or was there a slight

smirk to his lips when he asked the question? As if he was teasing her about something.

Maybe Marni was wrong to assume that he wasn't aware of their sleeping positions last night. She felt a slight heat creep up to her cheeks. Well, she certainly wasn't going to bring it up. She'd be horrified if she was wrong.

Besides, Gio was always teasing her in one way or another.

Better to just change the subject. "Too bad we're all out of those yummy pastries from yesterday." It wasn't as if she was lying, she wouldn't exactly turn down a croissant right now.

He shrugged. "We can always go get some more."

"Too wicked, isn't it? To have rich, sugary pastries two days in a row?"

Gio threw his head back and laughed. He winked at her when his gaze met hers again. "Darling, you and I have very different ideas about what we would define as *wicked*."

See, there it was. She was right. He only enjoyed teasing her. It was just his personality.

"Weren't you and Nella having junk food–laden movie nights not that long ago? I seem to recall walking into the viewing room at the house to find the two of you surrounded by snacks and candy. You didn't seem to think rich and sugary were wicked back then. What's changed?"

She ducked her head. He was too observant by far. "It's a rather recent habit. One I'm trying my best to unlearn."

Gio set his mug down. His eyes roamed over her face, full of concern. She shouldn't have given him such a loaded answer. Maybe one day she'd tell him about how Ander had even tried to control her eating habits. But she didn't have it in her right now.

Before he could ask anything more, she jumped off her stool and flashed him another wide smile. "You're right. I am on vacation and can have all the pastries I desire. Finish your tea and let's go get some."

Gio opened his mouth, clearly about to press her, but must have decided against it. He took a long swallow of his drink then offered her his arm. "Let's go."

He led her past the pool and patio area to the stone steps leading to the beach.

"What a gorgeous morning," Marni remarked. It was the truth. Crystal blue water crashed gently against golden sparkling sand in soft waves. A bright, round sun sat majestically above a cloudless horizon. As far as small talk went, it was a handy topic.

What she really wanted to do was ask him

about the obvious limp he was trying so desperately to hide. And if it had anything to do with his nightmares and tortured sleep. He must have forgotten how well she knew him after all these years. The Gio she remembered from before this trip was characterized by a flurry of activity. He'd always been a man who moved quickly, never one to sit still or stroll leisurely, no matter the circumstances. That version of Gio would have challenged her to a race down the beach.

How could he think she wouldn't notice the difference?

So maybe he'd overdone it with the amount of pastries he'd ordered. Two of everything the stand offered might have been a bit much.

Silently, he handed Marni another biscotti after she'd finished the sugared almond croissant. She sat on a big boulder, her legs dangling inches off the ground while he leaned his back against it. Gio tried hard to focus on his breakfast but it was hard not to stare at Marni. Her hair had come loose, that all too enticing shoulder remained exposed and there was a smidge of powdered sugar above her lip. It took all the will he had not to reach over and rub it off with his thumb. Or maybe with his mouth.

Instead, he silently handed her a napkin from

inside the box. She dabbed at her lips and the smidge disappeared. Thank God for lessened temptation.

A seagull flew overhead, past sandy beach and over the water. Marni shielded her eyes, watching its flight. She sighed deeply. "I know I keep talking about what a beautiful morning it is, but it really is picture-perfect. Like something out of a painting."

"I can't recall a single day it's rained in the week since I got here."

"You were right, Capri is paradise."

"It really is. I'm actually thinking of getting my own place here." He hadn't even realized he'd meant to share that with her.

She snapped her head in his direction. "How exciting, Gio! I think you should do it."

He bit down on the last of his biscotti, licked the crumbs off his thumb. "Nella mentioned a villa that's up for sale right now. Maybe we can look at it together."

Her mouth formed a small O in surprise. "I'd really like that. Just say when."

He couldn't quite place why, but somehow the moment had grown heavy. Something pivotal had just happened. Though he wouldn't be able to articulate why. Other than the understanding there was something rather intimate about viewing houses together. Something personal.

Gio gave his head a shake. He was being ridiculous. Two friends checking out a villa one of them might buy was purely platonic. Why in the world was he overanalyzing everything all of a sudden when it came to Marni?

"That was delicious," she finally declared after several more moments of chewing, steering the conversation back to lighter fare. "But I think I need to work off some of this sugar high."

Bouncing off the boulder, he watched as she removed her sandals and rolled up her capri pants to above her knees. Then she skipped, actually skipped, toward the water. A chuckle rose out of his chest at the image.

"You coming?" she asked with barely a backward glance.

He couldn't think of a single reason not to.

Kicking off his own sandals, he followed her into the crashing waves. She playfully kicked a splash of water in his direction when he reached her side, just enough to wet the bottom trim of his sports shorts.

"Why, Miss Payton," Gio began in a mock-serious tone. "How utterly childish of you."

Her response was a hearty laugh while she did it once more, getting him wetter this time.

He didn't mind. It was a dry, warm and sunny day. The water felt refreshing on his skin. He tried to think of the last time he'd been on the beach, simply frolicking in the water. Not a single instance came to mind. Not even from his childhood. In his before life, he'd have dived into the waves and began a series of laps, pushing himself harder and harder with each one.

What exactly had he been pushing for all those times?

"I wish I'd brought a swimsuit," Marni said, though she seemed to be getting rather wet enough despite being fully clothed.

"We can always come back."

She nodded with enthusiasm. "Yes! Let's do that. But I don't want to leave just yet."

Neither did he. In fact, he could stand out here and watch her frolicking in the water for hours. The thought both annoyed and amused him. What would he be doing right now if Marni had never arrived at the villa? No doubt, he'd be sitting at Nella's patio table poring over a spreadsheet or making phone calls. He certainly wouldn't be kicking around on the beach after having gorged on pastries.

When he looked up again, Marni had rolled her pants up higher, clear up to the tops of her thighs. She was several feet deeper in the water, much farther away than where he stood near the sand. A particular large wave appeared out of nowhere at that very moment.

Marni seemed to lose her footing as it crashed into her legs. Gio's vision blurred. There was no way he could reach her if she toppled over and got dragged under the water. Was Marni a proficient swimmer? How did he not know?

His heart hammered in his chest as he leaped to try and reach her before she could fall. With his bruised leg and weakened arm, he might not be able to pull her out if she went under and got in trouble. He'd barely made it to her side when he realized that not only had she remained upright, she was bent over laughing, her shoulders shaking with mirth.

Relief surged through him but it was quickly replaced by fury. What if she *had* fallen, what if the wave had taken her under and she'd been caught in the current.

"Did you see that?" she asked him, with amusement dancing in her eyes.

"Yeah. I saw how reckless and foolish you just were." Gio spit out the words, both unable and unwilling to temper his tone. She could have gotten seriously hurt. Or worse. And he would have been nearly helpless to do anything about it.

Her brows furrowed together, confusion clouding her eyes. "What?"

"You could have fallen in the water, Marni. I don't know how strong the current is." He thrust a hand through his hair. "I can't even remember if you're a good swimmer."

A slight breeze blew over Marni's skin as she exited the water. Goose bumps rose along her arms and legs but she couldn't tell if it was from the cold or the sheer terror she'd just witnessed on Gio's face. He was a step behind her when she turned to face him.

"Gio. What just happened? What got into you?" She tucked a wet curl of hair behind her ear. "All those vacations to Cape Cod I took with your family. Those three times I tagged along to the Bahamas with you all. How can you not remember if I can swim?"

Gio huffed out a breath of air and closed his eyes. "I just got nervous in the moment, all right? I thought you might get hurt and I wasn't sure if I'd be able to—" He looked away, never finishing the sentence.

She reached for him then, placing her hand on his forearm. He honestly had been frightened for her. Not that she could surmise why for the life of her. "You had to know I wasn't in any real danger."

Only he clearly hadn't known. "I just—" He broke off again, at an obvious loss for words.

Marni found herself torn between genuine curiosity about what was going on with him and the need to be sensitive to his boundaries. If he didn't want to share with her what was causing all these changes in him, who was she to push?

"Look, never mind," he said, turning away. "Let's just forget it happened, okay?"

Right. Like she had any hope of being able to do that.

"I think we should head back now," he announced, then didn't so much as spare another glance in her direction when he walked away.

Marni clenched her hands tight at her sides. She had no reason to feel guilty about how the morning had suddenly gone so sour. She hadn't done anything wrong. She refused to accept the burden of responsibility when it wasn't hers to bear. She'd made a vow to rid herself of the habit when she'd left Ander for good. He'd blamed her for anything and everything that had gone wrong in his life or career. No more.

Whatever Gio had plaguing him at this juncture in his life—and she felt for him, she really did because he was obviously dealing with something major and life-changing—she just didn't have it in her to play the fall guy. Not anymore.

They walked the rest of the way in silence, only broken when Gio handed their remaining pastries to a young mother visiting the beach with her two toddlers. The children hopped up and down with glee when they dug into the box.

A pang of longing shot through her chest as she watched the scene. The mom looked harried and tired, but happy to be with her children. She didn't know if she'd ever have that. Not with the mess her last relationship had turned out to be. She mentally scoffed. What was it with her and her faulty judgment when it came to men? Look at her inconvenient crush on current company. It was wrong enough on the surface, given their past history. But especially now considering whatever was going on with Gio that had him acting so uncharacteristically.

When they reached the house, she didn't bother to let him know that she'd be heading to the shower to clean up and dry off. It would probably be better if they spent the day apart. Obviously, it had been a mistake to deviate from the original plan on day one: stay out of each other's way. Well, she knew better now. Another vow she'd made was to stop making the same mistakes over and over.

Marni took her time in the shower. The stall smelled of him, his aftershave, his soap. The woodsy scent of the shampoo he used. How many times had she imagined running her fingers through the mass of dark curls that fell over his forehead. How often had she resisted the temptation to lean closer to him and inhale deeply of the minty scent of that aftershave?

She was heading down a dubious path here. Maybe it was just as well that they'd had that little falling-out at the beach. It served as a stark reminder that she needed to keep herself in check when it came to Gio Santino.

Still, she couldn't help the temptation to reach for her new phone when she returned to the bedroom and noticed it was finally fully charged. She knew Nella's number by heart.

If her friend had wanted her to know what was really going on with her brother, wouldn't she have told her by now? Although Marni had to admit Nella might have been hesitant to burden her with her family problems given all that Marni had been dealing with the past few months. Maybe that's why Nella hadn't said anything about Gio.

Marni reached for the phone and dialed the first three numbers before she hesitated. Rubbing a hand down her face, she tossed it onto the mattress and plopped down on the edge. No, she couldn't do it. She refused to call her best friend to ask her to dish about her older brother. How middle school cringe of her to even consider it.

Besides, didn't it also say quite a bit that he didn't trust her enough to tell her himself?

An hour later, try as she might, she couldn't stand to stay in the room any longer. This was silly. They could stay out of each other's way but they would still need to be civil over the next few days. Besides, she was thirsty. Marni would simply acknowledge him if she did run into him downstairs, explain that she hadn't meant any upset, get her drink and go about her day. But when she reached the first floor, Gio was sitting on the armchair facing the stairs, as if he was waiting for her.

He spoke before she could tell him any of the things she'd decided on upstairs. "Nella tells me you're a good listener."

Gio motioned with one hand to the love seat opposite where he sat. Marni forgot all about her thirst as she made her way into the sitting room and took a seat. They must have jinxed the weather the way they'd spoken about it earlier, because now the sky had grown dark and cloudy, throwing shadows on the walls. It fit the current mood perfectly.

Gio blew out a breath before speaking. "I scared you that first day you arrived. And I know I just scared you again earlier this morning," he began.

"You were concerned," Marni offered. "I under—"

Gio held up a hand to stop her before she could continue. "Please, just let me get through this. Before I have a chance to change my mind."

Marni nodded in agreement, remaining silent. Looked like she might finally be getting some answers, far be it from her to hamper that.

"You know I'm active in the various charities that Santino Foods sponsors."

"Yes, I know." As soon as he'd graduated college and joined the family company, Gio had taken on the responsibility of running the many charitable functions the family global company supported. But what did that have to do with anything that was happening with him now?

"There's an annual event called the Mangola Rally. It's a race across eastern Europe ending in a small town in Turkey. Santino Foods was asked to sponsor a racer. We would donate money and draw attention to benefit a good cause, in this case, a refugee crisis organization." He stopped to rub a hand across his eyes.

Marni waited for him to continue, not daring to interrupt.

Gio went on, "Rather than sponsor someone, I decided I would participate myself. I'd gotten into racing cars a couple years back. Had even come in first in a few amateur motorsport events. Felt pretty confident behind the wheel. It was for a good cause. Plus, it sounded like fun. So I convinced the organizers I was qualified."

"You always were one to take risks," she offered, not surprised in the least that he'd opted to participate himself.

Gio flinched at her words. Marni wanted to suck them back in somehow.

"Well, it was one risk too many it turns out."

Oh, no.

"About the halfway mark, somewhere in the roughly terrained vicinity of the Austrian border, I lost control of the car."

Gio squeezed his eyes shut as he continued. "I don't even know what happened. I must have hit a boulder, or some other obstruction. The car was going much too fast because I had to be the one who came in first, as usual. I couldn't regain control of the car no matter what I tried."

Gio's hands were clenched tight against his thighs. A muscle worked along his jaw. She hated that he was reliving this, especially considering it was for her sake.

He sucked in a breath and continued. "I must have hit my head at some point, I blacked out. When I came to, the car was upside down."

She could guess the rest. "Oh, Gio. I'm so

very sorry." Try as she might, there was nothing else she could think of to say.

"One of the other drivers came upon us eventually and called for help."

Us? Had she heard him correctly?

"You weren't alone in the car?"

Gio went pale and a shadow crossed his eyes. "That's the worst part. I had a codriver in the car with me to navigate the route. A family man with small children."

Marni's blood grew cold. "Is he...?" She couldn't bring herself to finish the sentence. Lucky for her, she didn't have to.

Gio shook his head. "He survived. Thank God." He sucked in a gulp of air. "But there's a question as to whether he'll ever walk again. And that's on me."

The enormity of what he'd just told her registered in her mind. It explained so much, no wonder Gio was in such a state. The nightmares, the restlessness, the tortured look behind his eyes when he thought she wasn't looking. No wonder he'd come here and secluded himself from everything and everyone he loved.

Not only had he suffered a catastrophic accident that could very well have killed him, he blamed himself for destroying someone's life.

A shudder racked through her core. He could

have been killed. She felt shaken and unsettled at the realization. He'd been a constant in her life for so long, the thought of not having him in it made her want to weep. She'd been so clueless as to what he'd been dealing with. "I had no idea."

He nodded. "For Juno's privacy while he tries to recover, I did my best to keep it out of the papers and gossip sites. Only close family knew all the details. Luckily, the media lost interest except for a few initial reports. Until very recently, that is."

"Until recently?"

He nodded. "Unfortunately. And I need to figure out a way to make sure the details continue to stay out of the news cycle."

She tried hard to fight it—none of this was about her, after all—but a small, selfish part of her homed in on one undeniable truth: he hadn't thought to include her in that small circle of people he'd entrusted with the full story.

Gio couldn't bring himself to look at Marni's face as she took in all that he was telling her for fear of what he might find on her expression. At best, she'd look pitying and he couldn't handle that. At worst, she'd be horrified at what his carelessness had led to.

He cleared his throat to explain some more.

"So you see, that's why I panicked when I thought you might fall in the water and hurt yourself. I might not have been able to help you if you got in trouble. My left leg is shattered, I broke several bones, some of which are still healing, I wouldn't have been able to move too well."

Her chin lifted. "I wouldn't need saving. But I understand."

Good to know. He didn't need to tell her then that the agony of watching her get hurt while he was helpless to help would have broken what was left of his soul once and for all.

He finally lifted his gaze to meet hers. There was nothing behind her eyes but concern.

"Is there nothing they can do?" she asked. "About your friend?"

"I have him set up in a specialty hospital in his native Switzerland. They're doing all they can, cutting-edge treatments. I pray every day that they find a way to heal him."

She nodded solemnly. "And what about your leg?"

He didn't want to get into this now, wasn't in the mood for any lectures. But in for a penny and all that. "I've undergone three different surgeries. The next step is rehab, which was recommended I do in Chicago with a world-renowned team of professionals who specialize in injuries like mine. I'll need more surgery after that."

"When do you start?"

He shrugged, bracing himself for the inevitable fallout when he told her. "I haven't made the appointment yet."

To his surprise, Marni merely nodded. No words of consternation followed, no warning that he was being dumb or stubborn. Could it be that she actually understood why he might be putting off the inevitable? Might she be the only person in his life who understood that he was capable of deciding for himself when and how quickly he'd be able to heal?

For the first time in several months, Gio felt a lightness come over him. The anguish coiled in his gut since the accident loosened. As difficult as it had been to get the words out, he felt as if a heavy anvil was lifted off his chest. He hated when his sister was right. Talking to Marni had in fact lessened some of the burden. He'd seen no judgment on her face, no accusation whatsoever.

Gio felt lighter but also thoroughly worn and spent. The conversation had brought all the dark memories up front and center when he'd been trying so hard to keep them at bay.

As if to match his mood, the afternoon had grown considerably darker since Marni first came down the stairs. The bright sunny morning they'd spent on the beach seemed so long ago. Hard to believe it had only been a few hours since they'd returned. The sun wasn't shining now, no seagulls could be heard outside. A bolt of lightning suddenly flashed outside the window followed by a loud blast of thunder.

"What were you saying earlier about the lack of rainy days?" Marni asked, walking to the screen to slide it shut. She closed it just in time. Fat, heavy raindrops began falling from the sky before she'd had a chance to latch the knob.

"Guess we were due."

She lifted a shoulder. "Darkness and rain have to appear some time."

Despite the seriousness of the moment, Gio had to bite his tongue to keep from laughing. Had she really just made such a blatantly obvious metaphor?

Marni must have come to the same realization, the corner of her mouth lifted ever so slightly.

"Too much?" she asked, the smile lingering on her lips.

"I'll say."

She bowed her head in mock shame. "As reparation, I offer to throw together some lunch for us," she stated, then glanced out the window.

"Since it doesn't look like we'll be going out to eat this afternoon."

"Accepted."

"I'll cut up that baguette we picked up yesterday, throw it on a board with some cold cuts and that delicious mozzarella you have in the fridge. Do you mind grabbing a bottle of wine from Nella's rack downstairs? I'll replace it the next time we go out."

"Sure. Maybe for entertainment we can watch another episode of that Bollywood series." Huh, he had no idea he would suggest such a thing. Or that he'd actually thought about watching that show ever again.

Her eyebrows lifted toward her hairline. Yeah, well, he was pretty surprised at the suggestion himself.

"Sure, my tablet's in my room. I'll go get it before I pull the food together."

He wasn't sure how she'd managed it, but somehow he'd gone from suffering the crushing weight of memories of the accident, to looking forward to a relaxing afternoon watching a show while listening to the rain. And it was all Marni's doing.

He couldn't resist teasing her yet again. "But please try not to fall asleep again. You have a tendency to snore."

She turned on her heel to glare at him. "What?

How would you possibly know that?" He watched her eyes widen as the realization dawned on her.

"Why you sneak," she threw out, her hands on her hips, though there was no bite in her tone.

"Why whatever do you mean?"

She pointed a finger in his direction. "That night, on the lounge chairs. You knew the whole time. Pretending you were clueless."

He crossed his arms over his chest. "Miss Payton, I have no idea what you are talking about."

"Right. Sure, you don't."

He laughed in response. "Go get your tablet. I'm dying to know what happens after the last dance battle."

CHAPTER SIX

THE NEXT MORNING Marni awoke to a noise she barely registered. Sunlight poured through the half-open blind on her window. She hadn't gotten much rest. It felt as if she'd just fallen asleep moments ago. How was it possible that it was morning already? She'd been plagued by disturbing dreams involving fiery crashes and being trapped in a car after it flipped. If simply hearing about Gio's accident had invaded her dreams, she couldn't imagine how nightmarish his nights must be.

Vaguely, she recalled a late-night disagreement about who would get the bed. The new furniture had yet to arrive, delayed by the freak storm yesterday. Both had insisted the other get the bed and room. She'd won by losing. Or maybe she'd lost by winning. Hard to tell. Gio wouldn't budge, insisted on sleeping on the couch.

Her heart ached for him and all he was dealing with. Maybe she'd been too quick to try and lighten the mood yesterday after he'd told her everything, but she would have given anything to help ease the pain so evident in his face.

There was the noise again. She finally recognized it as knocking. With a groan, she sat up. Why in the world was Gio knocking on her door first thing in the morning?

"Come in."

The door creaked open about a foot and Gio poked his head in. "You decent?"

"I said come in, didn't I?"

He shrugged, stepping into the room. "Didn't want to assume, sweetheart."

The endearment shot through to her center. It was way too early to be hearing sweet nothings from Gio Santino. She hadn't even had any caffeine yet.

"Sorry to wake you," he said. "But I waited and you didn't come down. And we only have a small window."

She blinked at him. "Gio. What in the world are you talking about?"

"The management agency called early this morning. About the villa that's available to buy. They said a rep can be there to let us in until about noon. If you'd rather go back to sleep, I understand."

Noon? Marni glanced at the bedside clock

for the first time. It was approaching ten thirty!
She couldn't recall the last time she'd slept so
late.

"Of course, I'll be down in a fast minute."

Gio's shoulders seemed to drop three inches
and he grinned. "Great. I'll see you in a bit."

He appeared relieved that she didn't turn
him down. And he'd waited for her instead of
just heading to the villa by himself. Did he
value her opinion that much? Or maybe he just
wanted her company. Either way, she couldn't
help the sense of pleasure that pulsed through
her.

In her line of work, she visited houses all the
time. So why was she practically feeling giddy
about visiting this one with Gio Santino?

He was waiting on the patio for her. "It's just
up the coast, past town," he informed her.

So another boat ride, then. The sky was clear
and blue once again. As if yesterday's storm
had never happened.

When they boarded, Gio once again handed
her the life jacket. She took it without question this time. Another piece that made more
sense now. Gio's adamant insistence that she
wear it the first time they'd sailed up the coast
the other day.

Now she studied his profile as he steered the
boat. Without warning, he turned his head in

her direction. Great. She'd been caught staring. *Gawking* might actually be a better word for it.

"What?" he asked, his smile warm and friendly.

No way she could tell him the truth about what she'd been really thinking. "I was just curious about manning a boat. Do I refer to you as captain while we're on it?"

He gave her a mock salute. "I like the thought of you referring to me as your captain."

So he was back to the teasing, flirtatious version of himself Marni was so familiar with. After what she'd leaned yesterday, she would take it. Not that their situations even compared, but it seemed the past year had been life changing for them both.

"Come here," Gio said, motioning her over to his side. "Give it a try if you're so curious."

She stood without hesitation. "You mean I can be the captain for a bit?"

"Let's not get ahead of ourselves."

Marni stood in front of him and gingerly took the wheel. The unexpected vibration threw her off for the first second. He left one hand on it as he helped her to steer. "Steady, we're just gonna keep going straight for a bit."

Marni could feel the strength of the water through her fingertips as she guided the boat over it. The cliffside rose majestically out of the ocean to their left, giving her the feeling of being yards below civilization. Which she supposed would be an accurate description. Sailing the ocean in Capri felt nothing like driving on land.

She hadn't even noticed until that moment that Gio had removed his hand off the wheel.

"You're a natural," he said into her ear.

That enticing scent of mint and sandalwood drifted to her nose. Even through the life jackets, she could feel the warmth of his body against hers. Her breath caught in her throat. Between the headiness of sailing the boat and the effect of Gio's proximity, her senses were in overdrive.

Finally, Gio reached for the wheel. "I should probably take it from here. We're almost at the shoreline."

Marni reluctantly let go and stepped away. As soon as she got her life sorted and figured out her next career move, she might have to see about sailing lessons back in the States.

Not that anything would compare to what she'd just experienced. For one thing, no lesson was going to feel the same as having Gio guide her.

It wouldn't even come close.

Gio had been looking forward to touring the villa more than he could explain. That had everything to do with Marni. In fact, if she wasn't here in Capri with him, he probably would have sent a representative and asked for pics. After they docked, he guided Marni up the stone steps to the property where a realty agent who introduced herself as Angela let them in.

She led them to the main sitting area first. "I think this would be an ideal vacation home for a couple such as yourselves," she said, her smile wide.

Marni's hand flew to her chest as she began to correct the other woman. "Oh! We're not—"

Gio interrupted her protest in Italian, quickly changing the subject. A germ of an idea forming in his mind. He and Marni certainly made a convincing picture of a couple touring a home they might share. Cupping Marni's elbow, he motioned for the agent to lead them through the area.

After a quick tour around the rest of the house, Angela allowed them some time to observe the villa alone.

"Well, what do you think?" he asked.

They were standing in what would be his sitting room if he made the purchase. It was spacious with high ceilings and a shiny polished hardwood floor.

"I think you're lucky to be able to afford this. This place is gorgeous."

He would have to agree. Gio never forgot that

he'd been born under a lucky star. He was the first son of a prosperous family, who'd managed to grow his own personal wealth. He'd often wondered if he deserved his good fortune. Especially over the past few months.

Marni continued, walking the length of the wall. "I mean, it's roomy and allows in a lot of light. I can think of all sorts of ways to decorate." She turned on her heel to face him, biting her lip. "That wasn't meant as any kind of plea that you hire me. I hope you know that. I'm just making observations. I hope you understand." She seemed genuinely concerned that her innocent statement might have landed wrong. Gio wanted to strangle the person who had done this to her. At times such as this one, she seemed horrified that she'd made some kind of mistake.

"I understand completely." She might not have meant it as a plea, but he would certainly consider it an offer. Of course he would. Who else would he get to help him furnish this place if he bought it?

A look of relief flushed over her features and she continued walking, trailing her fingers along the wall. When she got to the corner of the room, she tilted her head, studied the wall. "There appears to be a gap here, in the wallpaper. Though why anyone would wallpaper these days is beyond me."

She glanced toward the door, as if on the lookout.

"Something wrong?" Gio asked.

"I just want to see what's under this paper, there's some kind of pattern. Let me know if you see the agent approach. I don't want her to think I'm trying to tear the paper off."

Gio had to laugh. Somehow their visit to see an available property had turned into some kind of covert operation. Everything he did with Marni seemed to take on a special or unusual turn. Life was going to seem so flat and boring after they parted ways.

"I've got you covered," he assured her, his eyes trained to the door.

He heard the scrape of her fingernail. "Oh, my God," she said breathlessly a few seconds later.

"What is it?" Gio gave up on guard duty and strode to her side. She was picking at a spot on the wallpaper that had partially come off.

"If I'm not mistaken, there's a genuine mosaic under all this paper. Probably handcrafted."

Gio had no idea what that might mean. Was it a good thing?

"When did you say this place was built?" Marni asked.

He hadn't, it hadn't come up before now. "I think the details online said late nineteenth century."

She tapped the paper back in place and stepped away, her eyes alight with enthusiasm. "You could have a real work of art under all this. I can't imagine for the life of me why anyone would cover it up with plain beige wallpaper."

He wished there was a way to bottle up her excitement. He couldn't remember the last time he'd been so affected by a discovery. Let alone a wall. Maybe that was why he kept looking for ways to take risks. Just to be able to feel things the way someone like Marni did.

He recalled the way she'd reacted when he'd let her steer the boat. Such a mundane task as far as he was concerned. But Marni had been practically buzzing.

"I would kill to see what the entire thing might look like under that paper," Marni added.

He could only think of one way that would be possible.

"I wonder what other delightful discoveries a place like this might hold," she said, palming the wall with a faraway look on her face.

Gio figured she just might find out.

Angela's words echoed through his head...*a couple such as yourselves.*

Gio pushed the thought away. For now.

Twenty minutes later he and Marni were sitting outside on the vast patio by a sparkling blue infinity pool. The realty agent had locked up the house and left, asking them to shut the locked gate once they left.

The pool area felt like a mini paradise, complete with marble statues of cherubs and a plot of colorful flowers in each corner. Marni took her shoes off and sat at the edge of the pool, soaking her feet up to her ankles. The image looked right to his eyes, as if she belonged here.

As far as property went, it wouldn't be a bad purchase. He'd wanted a place in Capri for a while now, ever since his sister and husband had inherited their estate. He could picture himself lounging out here by the pool. Could picture having his morning espresso while seated at the bay window overlooking the cliffside. Funny thing was, in none of those pictures was he alone. The woman splashing her feet in the pool was central in every single one.

What that might mean for his psyche, he didn't even want to analyze. So much in his life was in turmoil right now. Marni was at a daunting crossroads herself. He had no business envisioning her in any part of a future he was so uncertain about.

Marni reached in the pool and cupped a

handful of water then splashed his legs with a playful giggle.

One thing he was certain of, regardless of what the future held, Gio planned to be the next owner of this villa.

Marni sighed and took another look back at the villa they'd just toured. The place really was rather remarkable. What she would give to use her skills to decorate a place like that. Who was she kidding? Even if Gio did buy the place and hire her to decorate it—and those were pretty big ifs—she'd have to do it virtually from thousands of miles away in the States. She couldn't stay here in Capri long term. She had to get back and see about putting her life back in order.

Still, a girl could dream.

"Are you in any rush to get back to Nella's?" Gio asked from the bow without looking away from the horizon.

"Not particularly," she answered. "Why?"

"There's something I want to show you. If you're up for it."

His wide smile of enthusiasm was enough for her.

"Sure."

Gio turned the boat in the other direction and ramped up the speed. Within half an hour they

approached a cavernous opening on the cliffside. A slew of motorboats, small yachts and
rowboats surrounded it in the water.

"Let's hope the wait won't be too long," Gio
said, then picked up his cell to make a phone
call. She couldn't make out any of the Italian.

"What exactly are we waiting for?" she asked.

"You'll see," he answered with a mischie-
vous gleam in his eyes. "Have some patience."

Moments later, Gio got a phone call and ma-
neuvered their boat around the other craft. One
of the men in the rowboats close to the cavern
opening was waving them over. Gio navigated
to his side then turned off the motor.

"Let's go," he told Marni, offering her a hand
then helping her onto the rowboat before jumping on himself.

"This is Mario," he introduced, "he'll be our
tour guide and rowboat driver."

Tour guide?

Marni cleared her throat. "Wait. Are you telling me we're about to sail into that massive
cave in the cliff wall?"

"That's right. This is the Grotta D'Abruzzo.
Wait till you see what it's like inside."

Excitement mixed with fear churned in
her chest. She'd never been great at closed-in
places. Exploring a water cave wasn't exactly
what she'd had in mind when she agreed ear-

lier to this outing. But Marlo was grinning and gesturing for them to be seated.

Marni swallowed her trepidation and sat down on one of the rungs. Then jolted in surprise when Gio took the one behind hers. Not so much because he'd sat behind her, but because of the closeness of their bodies in the small space. Her bottom was nestled against his inner thighs, his chest close against her back.

Suddenly, her trepidation about entering the cave was completely overtaken by the fire that shot through her system at the close contact.

Heat crawled over her skin, her nerve endings afire with the intimacy of their positions. Surely, Gio had to feel it too. She was practically sitting on his lap, for God's sake. His legs spread out, tight against her hips.

She froze when he leaned in to murmur in her ear, "Comfortable?" Marni didn't imagine the mischief in his tone. His breath felt hot against her cheek, tickled her earlobe. How in the world was she supposed to answer that?

Marni closed her eyes, willed herself to focus on her breathing.

Gio leaned into her shoulder once more. "Breathtaking, isn't it?"

Oh, she was breathless all right. But no doubt he was referring to whatever was in the cavern.

Marni opened her eyes and blinked when she focused on the view before her.

Was she seeing things? The cave was alight with a bright neon blue. The water below them glowed, the rock walls glittered indigo. It was as if they'd entered a monochrome painting that somehow lit up from the inside.

"Oh, my," was all she could muster in response.

"Quite a sight, huh?" Gio asked, his chin bopping against her bare shoulder.

"I've never seen anything like it. What is this place?"

"They say it used to be the private swimming hole of Emperor Tiberius of the Roman Empire." From the corner of her eye, she saw him point upward. "His castle was built above us."

"How is it lit up in blue fluorescence?"

She felt him shrug behind her. "I'm not sure about the exact physics." He asked Marlo a question in Italian. The other man replied with several accompanying hand gestures.

Gio translated when he was done. Something about holes in the cave wall and capturing the sunlight through the openings. But God, it was so hard to concentrate between his closeness, the feel of his breath against her skin and the spellbinding sight before her.

"Imagine having this as your private swimming pool," Gio said after several minutes spent simply admiring the view.

Marni could imagine it all too easily. Had the king come down here for a late-night skinny-dip with his queen? Had they stolen private moments in the water, surrounded by this heavenly light, simply enjoying the pleasure of each other's company? As well as other much more intimate pleasures?

The vignette morphed into more personal images in her mind's eye. Only now it wasn't the Roman king and queen she was picturing. Oh, God, it was her and Gio. What would it feel like to frolic in this water, in the dark, while held in his arms? To have his lips on hers in such a secluded and private setting? Heat rushed to her cheeks. She silently said a small prayer of thanks that Gio couldn't see her face.

No! For all that's holy. No, no, no!

Gio spoke again softly over her shoulder. "I see the sight has left you breathless," he said. "You're practically gasping for air."

If he only knew the truth.

His leg was angrily throbbing. Bolts of pain shot through his thigh down to his knee. It was almost bad enough that he could ignore the more constant ache in his side and rib cage. Almost.

He'd overdone it today.

A voice in his head wholeheartedly agreed. It listed the litany of things he'd done when he should have known better. Climbing stone steps, both at this villa and the one he would be buying. All that walking as he and Marni toured the property. Jumping into a rowboat.

That last one was probably the nail in the proverbial coffin. A perfect comparison since he felt like the pain might actually kill him if it didn't subside significantly.

"You're hurting, aren't you?"

He hadn't even seen Marni come out to the patio.

"What makes you say that?" he said in as light a voice as he could manage. It wasn't easy.

She lifted an eyebrow. "Oh, just the way your face is scrunched up as if you're pushing a heavy boulder up a steep cliff. Or maybe how you keep rubbing the spot above your knee. All sorts of clues I'm sharp enough to pick up on."

That was the problem. She was too sharp by half.

"It's nothing, Marni," he said with a forced chuckle. "Nothing a night's rest won't help. I'll be much better in the morning."

"But you haven't been getting any kind of good rest, have you?"

Well, she had a point there. He should have come up with a better way to assuage her.

"I'll be fine," he repeated, for lack of anything else to say.

"We did too much today. I wondered what you were thinking, jumping onto that boat."

Yeah, the thing was, he hadn't been thinking at all. Just anticipating the joy he might bring to Marni by taking her to the grotto. He was certainly paying for it now.

She walked over and sat down on the lounge chair next to him. "I just wish the new furniture would get here already."

"Hopefully soon. Though things tend to move slower in Europe. Especially this time of year, during vacation season."

Marni's spine straightened and she lifted her chin, as if she was prepping for a fight. "Listen, Santino. If you think for one minute I'm going to take the bed tonight while you try to sleep on the couch or this lounge chair or on a bunch of cushions, you better think again."

Gio rubbed a hand down his face. How often were they going to go through this? Although, this time, he was actually tempted given the thousands of small knives stabbing his leg muscles at the moment.

"I will not argue about this. It's settled."

"Marni—"

"No!" Her tone was sharp enough that he was somewhat surprised. "I said it's settled. In fact, if you don't take the bed, then I won't either. We'll both be uncomfortable while there's a perfectly good bed upstairs sitting empty."

He tried to argue, but found he just didn't have it in him. The pain medication he'd been given left him groggy and disoriented, a sensation he'd hated. And Marni was right, the thought of trying to endure this pain while lying horizontal on anything other than a mattress would no doubt result in a night of absolute agony.

"All right," he said, blowing out a resigned sigh.

"Don't you—" She stopped. "Wait. Did you just agree?"

He nodded. *"Sì. Hai vinto."*

Her eyes roamed over his face. "Huh. I win, huh? That tells me how much you must be hurting."

"Because I actually agreed with you?"

Marni shook her head. "No. That you reverted to speaking Italian."

"Okay. I admit. My leg doesn't feel real great right now. But I don't see why you have to sleep down here."

Marni practically rolled her eyes. "I knew

that was too easy. I thought you just said you agreed that you should take the bed."

"I did. But I think you should too."

Her eyes grew wide and her brows lifted clear to her hairline. Her shocked expression made him chuckle out loud. "Marni, it's a very large bed. And I'm hardly in any position to—"

She held her hand up to stop him. "I see what you're getting at. And you're right. We've both had an enjoyable yet tiring and long day. There's nothing wrong with two old friends getting a good night's sleep on the same mattress. Not much different than all those slumber parties Nella and I had at your house."

Gio's ego took a bit of a hit with that one. But she was right. For the most part. "Can we do each other's hair and paint our nails? Write in our journals?"

She nodded. "Sure, we could do all that. Or we could watch another episode of *Lotus Dreams*."

"That works too."

"Sounds like a decent plan to me. I'll go cue it up on the tablet."

"Can't wait." He was aiming for a sarcastic tone but realized he actually was looking forward to the night they'd just planned. Something about watching a mindless television show with Marni by his side was more appealing to him these days than a night out on the town. Or a night scuba diving or parasailing or dirt biking…or any of the countless, rather extreme ways he'd been entertaining himself throughout most of his adulthood.

"Before I do that, I'll go get you some ice for that leg."

There wasn't enough ice in the kitchen, maybe in all of Capri, that would do any good given the condition he was in right now. He was about to tell her not to bother, but she'd already left to go get it for him.

CHAPTER SEVEN

MAYBE THIS WASN'T such a great idea. Gio sighed as quietly as possible so as not to disturb Marni. He desperately wanted to toss and turn but didn't want to risk waking her. One of them should be able to get some shut-eye. They'd just retired half an hour ago. It was sure to be a long night.

"It's okay…"

He heard Marni's soft voice in the dark.

"I know you're not asleep."

"Are you?" The ridiculous question garnered a low laugh out of her.

"Guess," she answered.

Gio chuckled and turned to her. He'd been so concerned about moving toward her in his sleep that he was practically on the edge of the mattress. There was a good three feet of distance between them. "I'm sorry, for keeping you up."

She released a breath, turned over onto her back. "You're not the reason I haven't drifted off. I have a lot to think about and I can't seem to shut my mind off."

Boy, could he relate. It was better for both of them to just do their best to fall asleep. So he surprised himself when he opened his mouth to ask the next question. "What was it about him?"

Gio sensed her discomfort at the question. Finally, she turned her head to face him. "I don't exactly know why. I can only say that he was very charming at first. Until he wasn't."

"Tell me."

She was silent for so long, he figured she had no intention of sharing. Finally, she sighed and began to speak. "I told you about leaving my job, you remember?"

He remembered every bit of their conversations. Something that tended to happen when he truly enjoyed someone's company. "I do.

"All because you broke things off with your former…" He hesitated. He couldn't seem to use the word *lover* when it came to Marni's past relationship. Referring to her as someone else's lover felt wrong on his tongue.

"With your ex?" he finished.

"You do remember. Only I didn't just work with him. I worked *for* him."

"He had the nerve to fire you for breaking up with him?"

"More or less an accurate assumption."

A bolt of rage shot through his chest for a man he'd never laid eyes on. The damage he'd done to Marni was unforgivable.

"What would make it more accurate?"

"He was one of the head architects at the firm I worked for. Interoffice relationships weren't explicitly forbidden but everyone knew they were frowned upon by the higher-ups."

"I see."

"I got lots of disapproving glances and a few outright glares by the other partners."

Gio shook his head. It took two to be in a relationship. "That's pretty unfair."

"Then there was all the snickering and gossip from the other decorators. I could just guess what they were saying behind my back every time I was assigned a job."

He could also guess.

"That I slept my way to getting the assignment," she confirmed.

Again, wholly unfair. But it was the way of the world, wasn't it? Unfortunately, women were the ones who were often the target of bitterness in scenarios such as the one Marni was in. Kudos to her for having the good sense to remove herself from such a toxic situation.

Only, she hadn't walked away unscathed, without any battle wounds.

"What happened?" Gio prompted. He had

the feeling it would do her good to get some of this off her chest. And maybe it was selfish of him, but he had to acknowledge it did him a bit of good as well to focus on someone else's woes for a while. If that was indeed self-serving, at least it was a win-win.

"I knew I had to end the relationship. Between the way it was affecting my work environment and the way Ander…treated me. It was all too destructive to my well-being."

"How so?"

"He tried to control what I wore, how I dressed. What I ate, how much I ate. And nothing I did was ever enough to please him."

"Do I have to take a trip back to Mass?" he asked, completely serious and more than willing to do just that. "To pay this guy a visit?"

Marni puffed out a breath of air. "He's not worth it. Believe me. I would much rather just forget he existed."

That was fine with him.

Marni continued, "Only, that's proving hard to do since I was fired on his behalf."

"On his behalf?"

He felt her head bop up and down in a nod. "Ander wasn't happy about the breakup. He didn't try to hide it. In fact, he made sure the tension was thick and heavy every time we had to be in the same room together."

"Not exactly conducive to a work setting."

"Nope. He didn't care, he knew he could get away with it."

"And you were the one who ended up paying for it." Job or no job, Gio believed wholeheartedly that she was better off far away from that sorry excuse for a man.

"That's right," Marni said. "Out of nowhere, I was told they needed to do some cost cutting and could do with one less decorator. Never mind that I had seniority over two of the other decorators who got to stay."

Gio swore in Italian.

Marni repeated the epithet with a thick American accent, earning a guffaw out of him.

"I reached out to colleagues for other opportunities right away. But got a lot of cold-shouldered responses. I guess the gossip was too much for me to overcome. I am persona non grata right now in the Boston interior design scene."

"I'm really sorry, Marni," he said, his heart breaking for her.

"So now, thanks to Nella, I have two weeks to try and put it all behind me."

"If I know my sister, she insisted."

"You would be right," Marni said with a laugh. "But she only has my best interest at heart. And she's smart—what better way to regroup than to do it in paradise?"

He had to agree on that score. It was why he was here in Capri too, after all.

Marni had been through so much. Was still dealing with the vengeful manipulations of a jilted lover. The same nagging thought in his head since they'd toured the villa for sale resurfaced once again. It was hairbrained and ridiculous and nonsensical.

But maybe, just maybe, it might be a way to address both their dilemmas.

Who would have thought she'd be grateful for a bout of insomnia? Marni glanced at the digital clock behind Gio on the bedside table. They'd been simply lying there in bed, just talking, for over an hour. She'd had no idea just how badly she'd needed to purge herself of all that had happened in the past few months. Gio was a good listener. He offered no judgment, didn't pretend to know any of the answers. He simply listened quietly. Turned out, that was exactly what she needed right now.

Nella had been there for her, of course. As always, she was only a call away and checked on her often. But she had her own life to live, now as a newlywed no less, and Marni hadn't wanted to burden her. As for her mom, well, her mom was just too tired these days to care.

"What do you think you'll do?" he asked her now. "When you get back after the two weeks?"

That was the question, wasn't it? She had no plans other than to keep reaching out to people she knew in the field, sending out her CV and hoping for the best.

Except for those times when that one other option floated through her brain. But that was mere fantasy. How she would attempt to pull it off, she had no idea. Didn't even know where to start.

So she surprised herself when she answered Gio's question the way she did. "Well, during more wishful moments, I fantasize about branching out on my own. If I can figure out how."

"Like opening up your own place?"

"Yeah. But it's a big *if.*"

"Marni, I think that's a great idea."

She rubbed her forehead. "I don't know. It would be a lot. I'd have to figure out how to finance it. I'm barely scraping by as it is."

"There are ways to find investors for this kind of thing. Plus, you can start small."

Valid points. Her credit history was pretty good. A small business loan from the bank wasn't out of the question. But what if she failed? Again.

Then she'd be jobless and further in debt. Her school loans were enough to keep her finances in the red for years still.

"Let's pretend you have all the logistics figured out," Gio suggested. "What would you call the business?"

Marni's gut tightened at the question. She was nervous even pretending about having her own place, something she'd wanted so badly for so long. "Nothing fancy," she answered. "Probably Marni's Interior Design. Something along those lines."

"Where do you think you'd set up shop?"

Now that she'd voiced her pretend business name out loud, her stomach muscles loosened just a little. What was the harm in just pretending? "If I had to pick right now, I might say Somerville. Or Medford. Those towns are really growing fast right now. But not enough that I'd be priced out of leasing a place."

Huh. She hadn't even realized the thought had occurred to her.

"What kind of sign would you have above your door?"

"See, that's where I might get fancy. It would have to be big and colorful. With my name displayed cleaRLY in huge, artistic lettering."

The image flashed clearly in her mind as she spoke the words as if a physical sign hung before her at this very moment in the dark. So real, she thought she might be able to reach out her hand and touch it.

"What might your slogan be?" Gio asked.

She surprised herself by coming up with something right then and there. "Comfort, quality and personal attention guaranteed."

"I think that's perfect."

She kind of liked it too. "One of the things about working in such a large firm was not really knowing the clients enough to gage for certain exactly what they would find homey," she explained. "I never knew if I was creating a home interior that went with their innermost personality."

"With your own place, you can personally ensure that happens."

She slapped her palm on the mattress. "Exactly!"

Marni closed her eyes, now fully immersed in the make-believe world she'd just created—sitting at a big mahogany desk, speaking to a client, taking notes about how best to furnish their home. She couldn't guess how much time had gone by when she snapped her eyes open at a grunt from Gio. The moon cast just enough light in the room that she could see him gripping his thigh as well as clenching his lips. In fact, his whole body had gone rigid and tight. He was in pain still.

Marni cupped a hand to her mouth as a realization hit her. "I'm so sorry, Gio."

"What in the world are you apologizing for?"

"Here I am practically wailing about my misfortune then waxing poetic about my dreams. All the while you're lying there literally in pain. I'm being so selfish."

He chuckled. "You're hardly wailing. And you most definitely aren't selfish. Far from it. If anything, you've managed to take my mind off the pain for a bit."

If he really meant that, Marni was beyond grateful that she might have been able to provide even a small iota of comfort, albeit small, especially considering all he'd just done for her. For the first time since leaving the firm, she felt a glimmer of hope for her future. Maybe she'd never be able to start her own place, but the dream was enough to keep her afloat during the tough times.

"Thank you for that. And thanks for indulging in my fantasy design firm creation."

Though she'd be darned if it didn't seem just a bit more real now.

Gio reached over and tapped a playful finger to her nose. "You're welcome, gattina. Anytime."

She couldn't have heard him correctly.

Marni sat up on her blanket-size beach towel and shielded the sun from her eyes. Gio's shadow loomed large on the golden sand beside her. She'd spent the morning lounging by the water. Now he was here handing her a sweaty glass of lemonade.

And also apparently to make a suggestion that seemed too far-fetched to be real. "I'm sorry, I could have sworn you said that we should pretend to be a couple for the next several days."

He crouched down to one knee next to her, so close his scent mingled with the salty sea air. His forearm brushed her shoulder, raising goose bumps despite the heat of the day.

Focus.

"I must have heard wrong," she said now with a soft chuckle.

"Hear me out," he began. "I think a little pretense might be beneficial for both of us."

Marni studied his face, no signs of joking or humor in any of his features. He really was serious. "What kind of pretense?"

"We pretend we're here together intentionally. That we're dating."

Marni shifted in her position. "That settles it, no more of that Bollywood show for you. What you're suggesting sounds like a plot right out of its storylines."

"But it makes sense, gattina. We're seen doing the tourist thing together. Everyone assumes we're a couple. There's no speculation about either of us."

"Speculation?"

Gio sighed and sat down all the way next to her. "It must be a slow news week. Because there's a journalist for a regional publication who's been calling to find out more about the accident. My guess is that others will follow. For Juno's sake, I need to make sure to shut it down before it starts."

"So you want to pretend you're simply vacationing, but why the farce about us being together?" Marni had to swallow after uttering the last few words.

"This way, we avert any interest in digging up the past and give them something new and shiny to focus on. They'll drool at the human interest angle. A local CEO who narrowly avoided death and has now found love. One who's seen how tenuous and fragile life can be and wants to settle down and give up his playboy lifestyle."

"Huh."

"And you show the world that your previous relationship is well in your past."

His suggestion was still preposterous, but Marni was beginning to see the logic behind the plan. He didn't need to explain how it would be beneficial for her to have the world believing they were an item. It would certainly quiet down the rumors Ander was spreading about her. She would look like a woman who'd truly moved on. "You want it to look like you're simply on some kind of romantic vacation."

He tapped her nose playfully. "Right. What do you say? Do you want to think about it before you make your decision?"

Marni shook her head. "I guess it's worth a try. I mean, we have nothing to lose by giving it a shot."

Gio's grin in response had her insides quivering. "That's my gattina," he said. "All we need to do is just make sure to be seen around town, like we're on holiday together. Visiting attractions, playing tourist. It would settle down all the gossip about the both of us. No one really knows the true circumstances of why we're here except for Nella and Alex."

"How do we explain all this to them?"

He shrugged again. "If they even get wind of it, we'll just tell them the truth. That it's not real."

It's not real. Gio was merely suggesting they playact, put on a show for the rest of the world. So why was her mind flooded with images of the two of them together enjoying the sights and attractions of one of the most romantic places on earth?

Her mind knew it wouldn't be real. But her heart was already wishing it could have been.

Maybe Marni had been right. Maybe this idea was completely insane, a story straight out of the plot of a soap opera. Either way, Gio figured they had nothing to lose by giving it a try. A few leaks to some gossip sites, a few photos floating in the social media sphere, a well-placed comment here or there. That should be more than enough to still the wagging tongues on both his and Marni's behalf.

This dinner cruise along the Capri coast aboard a yacht was a good first stop. Judging by Marni's expression, she was enjoying herself to boot, which was icing on the cake. Wait until they arrived at their destination. She was sure to be stunned.

Speaking of being stunned, Marni's black wraparound dress draped over her curves and brought out her tanned skin. She'd done her hair up in a simple style that somehow made her look both elegant and casual. The woman sure did clean up well.

He'd instructed the captain to specifically have them go by the *faraglioni* rocks on their way to Il Faro, the famous lighthouse on the southern coast. This way, Marni could experience their majestic beauty as well as the lighthouse itself and its views. Just because they were on this outing for practical reasons didn't mean they couldn't make the most out of it. He could show her the beauty that was the Amalfi coast while they were at it.

Her jaw dropped when they approached the sight. "Oh, my," she whispered breathlessly.

He could hardly blame her wonder. The *faraglioni* rocks in Capri were one of the most captivating landscapes in the world. Towering out of the deep sea, waves crashing at their base with a beautiful view of verdant land in the distance.

"It's breathtaking," Marni added, not taking her eyes off the scene before them.

When the waiter appeared at their table to take their order, Gio fished his phone out of his pocket and handed it to the man. "Would you mind?"

Draping his arm around Marni, he pulled her closer to his side, the majesty of the rocks setting the scene behind them. "Smile for the photo, *cara*," he told her.

Taking his phone back, he glanced at the image on the screen. "Picture-perfect," he said to Marni. "This should work just fine."

Picture-perfect. Marni took a deep breath and tried to still the racing of her pulse. That's all this was, just a picture she and Gio were trying to project onto the world. One based on a complete falsehood. So why had her heart quickened when Gio put his arm around her and pulled her close? For his part, Gio seemed single-mindedly focused on their true objective—playing up their false relationship.

Well, she could do the same. She'd force herself to not be distracted by the scent of his aftershave or the way his silver-gray suit brought out the dark specks in his eyes and highlighted the darker streaks in his wavy hair.

No. She'd ignore all that and focus on the now. In the meantime, she'd enjoy this once-in-a-lifetime early evening dinner cruise aboard a luxury yacht.

The food arrived in short order, helping in her efforts at distraction. Fresh lemon dill sea bass and homemade pasta with a side of grilled vegetables. A few months ago she would have pushed the pasta aside, making sure to only eat the lean fish and veggies. All to maintain her calorie goal in case Ander asked.

What a relief not to have to worry about such things now. Marni's mouth watered. She wasn't sure what her expression must have held but when she looked up Gio was staring at her with concern.

"Is that not to your liking? We can ask for something else?"

"No, it's absolutely perfect," she answered, sticking her fork in the pasta first. "I can't wait for dessert."

Several minutes later, the boat gradually slowed as they approached a redbrick building. Atop it sat a tall lighthouse. They came to a stop just as a waiter appeared with a tray that held two silver goblets half-full of golden liquid. "For the viewing," he said in a charming Italian accent.

Marni took one of the offered drinks and sniffed. They nutty aroma of almonds and spice tickled her nose. "What exactly are we viewing?" she asked Gio after the server walked away.

But he simply winked at her then said, "You'll see."

"Why can't you just tell me?"

"Because there's no way to describe it, gattina."

Marni realized just how true that statement was once they'd disembarked and walked up a stone pathway toward the lighthouse.

"La Punta Carena," Gio announced. "The best place in the world to watch the sun setting over the Mediterranean."

Marni slowly sipped her drink and watched

the horizon as the sun began to lower in the sky. Gio's words had not been an exaggeration. The horizon was a striking hue of red and orange, the water beneath it sparkling like jewelry. It was like watching a live-action view of a masterpiece painting.

Pretense or not, this was one of the most breathtaking scenes she'd ever witnessed. One she'd never forget.

Sighing deeply, Marni leaned back against Gio's chest and simply enjoyed the view, surrounded by his scent and heat.

CHAPTER EIGHT

"I THINK WE'VE floated enough photos out there for this plan to work," Gio announced the next morning. She'd come out to the patio to admire the now familiar view of the ocean in the horizon past the infinity pool. She was going to miss this ritual when she had to return to Boston in a few days. "Combined with the leak that we were seen touring an available villa together, I think we've got a solid foundation for our fake relationship."

Why did she cringe inside every time she heard those last two words?

Gio continued, "But just in case, I've got one more outing planned for us this afternoon."

Marni lowered her sunglasses to study him. "Another outing, huh?"

Gio nodded, his smile growing. If she didn't know any better, she might think he was actually enjoying all this activity. Still, she'd been growing more and more concerned about whether he was overtaxing himself. He'd insisted on walking along the pathway at the base of the lighthouse yesterday so that Marni got the full experience. But she was loath to say anything to him. Gio seemed to take any hint at his vulnerability as some kind of affront.

She could only hope whatever he had planned for today wouldn't involve too much physical effort. For his sake.

"What kind of activity?"

"The Gardens of Augustus. No trip to Capri would be complete without a visit there." He plopped himself down on the lounge chair next to her. "And it will give us another chance to be seen out and about together. The gardens are usually full of visitors this time of year. It's a beautiful day so today will be no different."

Gio was proven right about the crowd size when they arrived by private car two hours later to the winding pathway that led up to the world-renowned botanical garden.

Marni made sure to walk as slowly as she could so that Gio wouldn't overwork his sore leg, taking several breaks along the way. The breaks weren't all that contrived, like the ones yesterday, these views were equally stunning, taking her breath away.

The park's layout consisted of different sections, each made to look like a terrace full of botanicals overlooking the coastline and ocean beyond. Grand statues dotted the landscape, as if a museum of sculptures had its pieces scattered throughout a magnificent garden. Marni had never seen anything like it. She was having trouble deciding exactly which visual feast she should focus her eyes on.

"What do you think?" Gio asked as they stood in a terrace full of colorful dahlias and luscious green leaves. Marble statues flanked them on either side, a cherub to the right and a maiden carrying a load of fruit on the left.

"I think I might have died and am right at this moment walking through Eden," she answered, the awe in her voice clear to her own ears.

A commotion sounded from the pathway a few feet behind them. Excited voices, male and female alike, speaking in what sounded like German.

Marni turned to watch as a bridal procession made their way past the terrace. Half a dozen tuxedoed young men walking alongside elegantly styled women in sapphire blue gowns. Trailing behind them was a bride clad in layers of white silk and delicate lace walking alongside her groom. The couple seemed totally engrossed in one another, oblivious to anything around them, including their own bridal party.

The scene could have been a picture straight out of a bridal magazine. What an absolutely idyllic venue for a wedding. How lucky these two people were, to have found love and were now able to celebrate it with a union bonded in paradise. A bubble of envy formed in her chest, mixed with longing. How could she ever hope to do the same given her disastrous romantic history?

She released a long sigh, which came out sounding much louder than she would have anticipated. Sure enough, when she turned her head, Gio leveled a curious look her way. Maybe it was irrational, but she found herself getting defensive.

"What?" she asked, her tone on the side of aggressive. "Is it so odd to appreciate young love?"

"Is that what you were doing, gattina? Appreciating?" He tilted his head, a slight smile to his lips. He was teasing her!

"Do you mean to tell me that you've never entertained the idea of your own wedding? Where it might be? Not even once?" She found herself asking, against her better judgment.

His smile grew smirk-like. "Oh, sure, we talk about it every time me and the boys get together. Then us guys draw hearts all over our notebooks and sign the names of our crushes on our palms."

"That's ridiculous."

Gio turned with a chuckle to face the view of the Marina Piccola in front of them, crossing his arms in front of his chest. "Fine. To answer your question, no I never gave much thought to my wedding. Or marriage in particular. There was never an occasion to."

So there'd never been a woman who'd inspired thoughts of marriage. Heaven help her, Marni felt a twinge of relief at that notion. Which made absolutely no sense whatsoever.

But she was deflated by the next words out of Gio's mouth. "Now I can't even entertain the thought. Not for a long while," he said solemnly, his gaze narrowing on the horizon.

"Why is that?" she asked. Again, probably another dumb question she didn't really want to hear the answer to.

He shrugged, his jawline tensing. "How could I even think of that? The state I'm in, on top of all my regular responsibilities, how could I even consider tying myself to another person?"

A lump formed in Marni's throat. She had no business feeling so dejected by his words. She was only his pretend girlfriend.

How silly of her to take any of it personally.

For the third time during the span of a week, Gio opened his eyes to the brightness of sunshine rather than watching the onset of dawn. He'd been able to fall and stay asleep. Despite the pain.

Marni. He had her to thank. Again.

As his focus continued to clear, he realized exactly why he'd slept so comfortably. She was nestled against him and he was holding her in his arms. Sometime during the night, Marni had shifted to his side of the bed. He must have instinctively wrapped his arms around her.

This is wrong. This shouldn't be happening.

His subconscious was simply blurring the lines, had lost sight of what was real and what was pretend. A whisper-soft voice in his head tried to tell him all this but he gave it no need. He made no effort to move or push her away. It didn't help that Marni had been asking him about matrimony and romantic marriage proposals just yesterday.

But…it felt right, lying next to her this way. The scent of her brought to mind roses and fresh berries. The warmth of her body spread over his skin, right through to his soul. The sunrays shining through the window behind her cast her in a halo of light. Several tendrils of her hair fell around her face. She was utterly enchanting. His fingers itched to reach for her, to gently caress those untamed curls. His gaze fell to her lips: full and rose red, puckered slightly in her slumber.

Not for the first time, he wondered what she would taste like if he kissed her. Sweet as honey, no doubt. With a touch of those berries he always smelled whenever she was near.

He sensed more than saw it when she opened her eyes. They widened in surprise before heat darkened their depths. She made no effort to move out of his grasp. And he wasn't even remotely inclined to push her away.

They were a hair's breadth apart. Her eyes roamed over his face and he nearly groaned out loud when they landed on his lips. Did she want him to kiss her, maybe even as much as he craved doing so?

The voice grew louder, more adamant. Repeating the warnings he was trying so hard to ignore.

"Gio?" She spoke softly, her voice low and thick. The sound of his name on her lips had something shifting in his middle. He gave himself permission to gently trail his fingers around the frame of her face, to tuck back a couple of those wayward locks behind her ear.

"Good morning, sweetheart."

Her response was to shift even closer, then tilt her face up toward his. Heaven help him, he wouldn't even have to move his head to take her mouth with his, to finally succumb to the longings he'd been pushing away for so long. A low hungry groan sounded in his ears and he realized it was coming from him. Just one kiss.

Stop. This. Now.

This time, the voice was too loud and too harsh to ignore. Because he could no longer deny how wrong going down this path would be for them both.

With all the will he could summon, Gio moved back away from her, then sat up. Her look of confusion had him cursing inside, made him yearn to return to her. To take those lips with his own the way he so badly wanted to.

But then what?

The possible answers to that question were much too dangerous to explore. What if they didn't stop with one kiss. A very real possibility given his body's reaction and the way Marni had been looking at him just now.

Summoning the last vestiges of his control, Gio turned to sit on the edge of the bed with his back to her. "I should get up. There are some emails I need to check on."

Not exactly a lie. For one thing, he wanted to check for any updates on Juno's recovery progress. For another, he was going to follow up on when that blasted bed might finally arrive.

The sound of her rustling behind him told

him Marni was getting up as well. He waited without breath in case she said something, tried to stop him.

She remained silent.

He should have been relieved. Instead he felt a heavy brick of disappointment settle in his chest.

He took his time to get showered and dressed but then there was no longer any reason to delay the inevitable. He would have to face Marni sooner or later. Damn him for not having the sense to turn her down about sharing the bed last night. He would have preferred an uncomfortable and pain-inducing night on the sofa. Too late now.

When he made it downstairs, Marni was curled up on the love seat, still wearing her nightclothes, her hair up in that too tight ponytail again. What he wouldn't have given to set it loose and run his fingers through the strands the way he had moments ago.

"Good morning," he said by way of greeting, then cringed. He'd already said that to her upstairs.

She didn't quite meet his gaze when she responded in kind. Gio swallowed a curse. This was exactly what he'd wanted to avoid. This awkwardness between them. She wasn't even meeting his eyes. So different from before.

They'd been so comfortable with each other last night, their conversation so easy.

Now the air was thick with the tension of all that was and had to remain unspoken.

Or he could just go sit next to her, take her in his arms and tell her honestly how badly he wanted to kiss her. Then he would oblige if she said she wanted the same.

No. That was the last thing he should do, as tempting as it was.

"I'm about to brew some coffee. Can I get you some?" he offered.

She shook her head.

"How about some breakfast?"

"No, thank you."

Gio went about the business of getting himself caffeinated and fed. Looked like things were going to remain awkward between them, for now, anyway.

Because he couldn't think of a darn thing to say to make it any better.

Were they just going to ignore what had almost happened between them?

It seemed so, Marni figured as she watched Gio go about his morning as if nothing had changed. He brewed his espresso, offered to make her one or brew some water for her tea, then moved to the patio with his phone to check on those all-so-important emails that he'd used as an excuse to rush out of the bedroom this morning.

While she was still shaking with desire inside. While she was still imagining what it might feel like to have his stubble rub against her cheek. While she longed to be in his arms once more.

When she'd woken up briefly to find herself wrapped tight in Gio's embrace, she'd stayed where she was wrapped in the cocoon of his warmth. He'd seemed in no rush to let her go.

Now Gio was behaving as if none of it had even happened.

Well, he had the right of it, didn't he? He was actually thinking straight as opposed to the way she was letting her emotions run rampant. It had to be their surroundings.

This was Gio. Nella's brother. She'd practically grown up with him. They'd always had an easy camaraderie, even during all those times she and Nella were being pesky little tagalongs. Surely, they could get back to that dynamic.

Marni scrunched her face and blew out a breath.

Who was she kidding? As if. Even now, she itched to run her hands over his chest, touch her tongue to his lips, ask him to wrap his arms around her the way he had last night.

All this pretending they'd been doing was blurring her reality, bringing to the surface all the attraction she'd tried so hard to curb.

So going back to the way they'd been before this trip was wishful thinking. Still, things between them couldn't remain as tense as they were. She still had eight days here before her return flight. She would need every one of those days to figure out what she intended to return to.

Marni had to forget about the almost kiss like Gio apparently had.

So when Gio finally left the patio to announce he wanted to take a walk along the beach, she didn't hesitate. "I'd like to come with you if you don't mind the company."

He quirked an eyebrow at her in surprise. "You sure? My leg's stiffening up just sitting out there. I might be kind of slow."

"A slow and leisurely stroll. Sounds perfect. Let me just throw some shorts and a T-shirt on."

He tilted his head. "Take your time."

He was waiting for her by the pool when she came back down dressed less than five minutes later.

He hadn't been kidding about being slow. It took him much longer to get down the stone steps this morning. Maybe they should have just stayed put or floated around in the pool rather than tax his already strained leg any more.

She was about to ask him when he spoke before she could. "Feels better already, just being out here by the water in the sunshine."

Why did she get the feeling he wasn't telling the entire truth?

Marni decided not to press, the whole point of walking with him was to overcome the awkwardness between them after the almost-kiss.

"It's beautiful," she agreed. "I wore my swimsuit underneath…the water looks pretty inviting."

So there was that bit of small talk out of the way, then. Now what?

"Have you thought any more about your pretend design business?" Gio asked as they made their way along the water.

Marni waved her hand in dismissal. "Oh, that was just a bit of fun on my part, answering your questions like that. None of it is real." *Like a lot of other things that may have happened last night*, she added silently.

"But it could be," Gio countered. "I thought we established that."

Marni stared out at the horizon. She knew Gio meant well, but dwelling on a pipe dream wasn't going to do her any good right now. She had to get practical and figure out a manageable path forward.

"Maybe," she finally answered. "But I think for now I'll stick with plan A or B. My own shop is probably more like plan Z in the overall scheme of things."

"Huh."

Was it her imagination, or did that one tiny sound hold just a hint of judgment? She felt a prickle of irritation.

Truce, she reminded herself.

"If I understood correctly last night, your plan A seems to be to keep looking for another job like the one you had."

And lost. "That's right."

"So what does plan B involve, then?"

She shrugged. "I thought maybe I'd travel to New York City to try my hand there. It's a much bigger market. With more opportunities."

"Is that what you want? To live in New York?"

Why was he asking her all these questions? This was supposed to be a stress-free stroll together to reestablish their friendship. She hadn't realized her very motivations would be poked and analyzed.

"New York is a thrilling place to live," she said noncommittally. "The Big Apple and all that."

"Yeah, but it's not your home."

She had to veer this conversation in another direction, away from herself. It was only fair to discuss Gio for a while. Besides, hadn't she shared enough about herself last night?

"What about you?" she asked.

"How do you mean? I'm still CEO at Santino Foods."

"I know that. But you have to admit the life you're going back to won't be the same one you left."

That was one thing they had in common.

Gio wasn't sure why but his pulse had quickened at Marni's words. The truth was, he hadn't really planned for much past this trip. For the first time in his life, he found himself focusing only on the short term. He just wanted to monitor Juno's recovery and continue pursuing his goals for Santino Foods. The company had a highly efficient and competent staff of employees. But with the loss of his father a decade ago and Nella having no interest in the business, the brunt of the responsibility fell on his shoulders. His mother did what she could to help, but with her advanced age she could only do so much. So many people depended on him for their livelihoods. He had a board of directors he had to answer to. Which just made his careless risk-taking that much worse.

Well, he'd learned his lesson.

"The only change I can be certain of is not participating in any more road races for the foreseeable future," he answered, squinting in the bright sunlight.

"I'm glad to hear it," Marni answered. "Nella will be too."

Gio didn't miss that she'd just put herself in the same context as his sister. That had to be intentional. If she thought that was going to make him forget his desire for her, they were way past that stage. He would just have to make the best of the new dynamic and try to ignore the inconvenient feelings he'd developed.

Easier said than done. He had to try. For both their sakes.

"What made you do it?" Marni asked the question completely out of the blue. "I mean, I know you've always been a bit of a daredevil. But why a charity race across rough terrain through several countries?"

He shrugged. "The organization it was meant to support was struggling to find participants that might draw the kind of attention and publicity they needed for the race to be successful."

Having the Santino name attached to the race had done a lot toward that end, but it wasn't enough. Not until he'd actually been announced as one of the drivers did they see big dollar amount donations.

"Ah, I get it," Marni said. "You knew that if the CEO of an international conglomerate was an actual participant, the publicity alone would bring in more money."

She'd always been clever.

He nodded. "That's right. And there were all those friends and colleagues who wanted to pay for the privilege of taunting me if I didn't win."

Marni laughed. "I'm sure in a very good-natured way."

Despite the seriousness of the conversation, the sound of her laughter lightened some of the heaviness in his chest. See, there was no reason to let any sort of awkwardness continue between them. They could continue as villa mates until she had to leave. He had to admit, he was going to really miss her company when she left in a few days. He probably wouldn't stay much longer after that himself.

The bright yellow tank top she wore cinched at the waist and brought out the golden specks of her irises. Her denim shorts showed off her shapely thighs. Thank God she wasn't wearing those plain leather flats today. The sandals she had on were much more enticing, showing off the bright pink polish on her toes.

When had he ever noticed a woman's toenail

polish before? Not a single time he could recall.
Maybe he wasn't completely over his concussion, after all.

He focused on the waves splashing near his
feet to get his mind to behave. "For the most
part," he said.

"So you had the most noble of intentions."

"I guess you could say that." He certainly
had in the beginning. The race seemed like
a fun way to support a good cause. But it all
went so terribly wrong. Now there was a young
man laid up in a hospital while he was in pain
every night.

She paused and touched his forearm. Gio
braced himself, certain he wasn't going to like
what was about to follow. "Gio, if you don't
mind my asking, what do the doctors have to
say?" She swallowed, clearly nervous about
asking the question.

He was right, he really didn't want to go
down this path of questioning. He shrugged.
"The normal doctorly stuff."

"What does that mean? And you don't have
to tell me if you don't want to."

Her bright hazel eyes clouded with concern.
How could he not give her something?

He shrugged. "Like I told you. There's at
least two more surgeries they say I need. But
the muscles need to heal first. In the mean-

time, they prescribe constant and regular physical therapy appointments. Which I'm sure will continue for the foreseeable future."

Marni's hand lingered on his arm. For a crazy second, he wanted to take it in his, lift it up to his lips and plant a gentle kiss on her palm. And wasn't this a fine time to be thinking of doing something so silly and inappropriate for the moment?

"I meant, what are they saying about when you should start the therapy. So that you can move forward with the surgeries."

He was supposed to start them a week ago but had canceled every single scheduled appointment. "When I get around to it. I'm not in any rush."

No need to tell her that decision ran completely against all the medical advice he'd been given. Or that the last surgeon had bluntly and unwaveringly told him that Gio was certain to make his condition worse by delaying the treatment.

But it was as if Marni could read his mind. Her lips thinned into a tight line, and her eyebrows drew together over those piercing hazel eyes. There was no mistaking the disappointment that washed over her features. Along with a solid dose of worry. It was the worry that annoyed him most. "You've been putting it off, haven't you? The therapy and the surgeries."

Like he'd thought earlier, the lady had always been very clever.

"There's no need to look at me like that," Gio said and resumed walking but at a much faster pace—which had to hurt his leg. And for what? Marni wondered. It wasn't as if he was going to get away from her on this beach.

She began to follow fast on his heels and caught up to him in a second. "Like what? How do you think I'm looking at you?"

"Forget it, Marni. Let's just turn around and go back."

A bit late for that. She slammed her hands on her hips. "No. I'd like an answer," she demanded, not even sure why she was pushing him this way. The conversation was getting way too heated. So much for that truce she'd been after. "So tell me."

"I don't know," he bit out. "Why are you badgering me? As if I've tried to drown your pet squirrel in that ocean or something." He thrust his thumb in the direction of the water.

In spite of her frustration with him at what she'd just learned, Marni's mouth quivered with the onset of a laugh. She squashed it. "Why in the world would I keep a pet squirrel?"

He turned to her then, rammed a hand through the hair at his crown. "Didn't you at some point or other have a small furry rodent? I remember Nella having to pet sit."

"That was a guinea pig, Gio. Completely different animal than a squirrel."

How in the world had they gotten so off topic anyway?

He crossed his arms in front of his chest. "Never mind. I suppose you're going to tell me, like everyone else that I'm being stubborn and stupid for not trying to get better as fast as I can."

"No, I wasn't going to say any of that. And I'm not going to ask you why either, for that matter."

Both eyebrows lifted and his jaw tightened. "You're not?"

She shook her head. "I think I can guess. Plus, I'm sure you wouldn't answer me anyway."

He narrowed his eyes on her. "You're right, I wouldn't answer. As for the first part, don't be so sure. You don't know me as well as you think you do."

Ouch. Marni sucked in a breath at the taunt. If he'd meant to be cutting and harsh, he'd hit the mark perfectly. Any trace of amusement flowed out of her. In her head, she knew he was just lashing out because he'd been forced to admit something he didn't want to share with her. But her heart did a little flip at the cruelty.

"Right," she said. "I suppose you're also going to tell me it's none of my business."

He reached for her shoulders, took them in a gentle but firm grip. "Don't put words in my mouth, Marni."

Her mouth went dry at the contact. This was so not the time to notice the fullness of his lips, the way his dark hair curled messily over his forehead, blowing about his face in the breeze. His dark brown eyes blazed with emotion. And something else. Something that had her blood zinging in her veins. Her heart began to pound in her chest.

She somehow got her mouth to work. "So you're saying you are my business, then?"

"I've known you a long time." His answer wasn't really an answer at all.

Suddenly, her own tenuous grasp on her emotions snapped like a dry twig. Marni knew she should step away, out of his grasp. Instead, she did the opposite. She moved forward until they were toe to toe, her face a mere inch from his. Marni knew she was playing with fire, but couldn't seem to help herself.

Once again, her mouth was within a hair's breadth from Gio's. But unlike this morning, there was nothing gentle about the way he was looking at her.

He looked like he could devour her on the spot.

That dangerous, wayward thought had her breath catching in her lungs. Gio noticed, because his lips formed a knowing smile. "What's the matter? Something wrong, gattina?"

Oh, God. Never before had the nickname sounded quite so sexy to her ears. She would never hear it the same way again after this moment.

Yes! she wanted to cry out. All sorts of things were wrong. Like how badly she wanted his lips on hers even though she was beyond angry at him for the way he was risking his health by delaying getting medical treatment. Or how much she wanted to thrust her fingers in his hair and bring his mouth down to hers. How disappointed she'd been that he'd left the bed this morning instead of just kissing her then.

She couldn't even be sure which one of them moved first. Maybe they both did. But suddenly, what she'd been fantasizing and dreaming about was somehow happening. Gio's lips found hers in a crushing, shattering kiss. His hands moved from her shoulders to wrap around her waist and pull her closer. Her hair was suddenly free from its binding with Gio's fingers threading her loose strands before pressing his mouth into hers harder.

She couldn't get close enough, wanted to feel the length of him even tighter up against her body. Good thing they were out in the open on a beach where anyone could walk by. Or Marni would have been unable to keep herself from tearing his shirt off to run her hands down his chest, over his washboard stomach. Then lower.

This was why he'd been smart not to kiss her in the bedroom earlier. She had no doubt she wouldn't have been able to stop herself from going further, as far as he would let her.

Marni leaned into him now, savoring the taste of him. His warmth seared her skin. Heat and longing curled in her belly and moved lower, and every nerve ending tingled with electricity. The world around her ceased to exist. Nothing mattered but Gio Santino and the way he was kissing her.

She never wanted it to stop.

CHAPTER NINE

How could he have lost control like that? Gio bit down on the curse that formed on his lips when he finally let Marni go. Which took way too long.

And he'd gone way too far.

He'd been naive to think they could simply gloss over what had happened between them this morning. Walking away from the bed this morning, rather than facing reality then and there, had only led to a slow simmering of tension between them that had just blown up in spectacular fashion. He had to figure out a way to put out the fire.

He dared to meet Marni's gaze now. His breath caught in his throat at the sight of her. Her hair fell in a mess around her face and shoulders, her lips were swollen. Her cheeks flushed berry red. God help him, she looked ready and waiting for him to do it again.

She looked like some sort of modern goddess, standing on the golden sand. The bright sun highlighted the streaks of golden bronze in her hair. The sparkling blue water of the ocean served as a background as if she were the center of some classic painting. Everything about her called to him, made him want her more.

How totally inconvenient.

It took several moments to get his mouth to work. "Marni, look, I'm so—"

She held a hand up to stop him before he could finish, her eyes ablaze. "Don't you dare finish that sentence, Gio Santino. Don't you dare apologize to me right now."

Gio rubbed his palm down his face. "What do you want me to say?"

She didn't answer, simply glared at him some more. Several beats passed by in silence, the air between them heavy. Gio clenched his fists at his sides to keep from reaching for her again, wiping that angry glare from her face with another deep satisfying kiss.

No! Enough already.

Kissing her again was the last thing he should be thinking about. Instead, he should be trying to figure out how they were going to get past this. Not just for this week but for the rest of their lives. Marni was practically family. They couldn't spend the rest of their days uncomfortable around each other just because he hadn't been able to control himself the brief period of time they'd been alone together.

Marni turned on her heel. "I think I'm done walking now."

Gio watched her retreating back as she made her way toward the house. He debated following her but the tension in her shoulders and the rigid set of her spine told him she wouldn't welcome his presence right now. Just as well, it was probably best for them both to be alone for a while.

Maybe for a long while at that.

Within minutes of docking the boat and arriving in town, Gio's phone vibrated in his pocket and he recognized his sister's ringtone. He pinched the bridge of his nose, not really up for a conversation with anyone right now let alone his chatty sibling. But guilt had him pulling out the device and answering just before it went to voice mail.

Her face appeared on the screen. "Hey, big bro."

Gio did his best to summon a smile and leaned back against the brick wall of a seafood store. Why did she have to place a video call now of all times? "Hey yourself."

Nella's eyes traveled behind him. "You're not at the house?"

"I'm in town for a couple of errands."

"Is Marni with you? She didn't answer when I called her just now. I wanted to speak to you both actually."

Again, she'd called her friend first. Not that he was offended in any way. It just confirmed what he already knew about their relationship. Nella and Marni didn't share any blood, but in every other sense they were true sisters.

Which only proved just how wrong it was to kiss her this morning. His sibling's soul sister should be completely off-limits, no matter how much he was attracted to her.

"Nope. I'm by myself."

Nella rested her chin on her hand. "Why didn't you bring her with you? Marni loves to shop."

He wasn't about to get into any of that. But Nella could be relentless about getting answers when she was curious about something. And she was like a bloodhound if she thought she detected a lie.

Gio really regretted answering the phone. He'd have to give her something. "I just had to come into town for a couple things. Just decided to do it by myself," he answered, hoping it was enough to placate her while still being vague.

No such luck. She straightened in her chair,

obviously not buying it. "Well, it was rude of you not to invite her."

Rude. Ha! As if that was the worst of it.

"She wouldn't have wanted to come." Mistake. It was the wrong thing to say.

Nella's head lifted with concern, the casual smile fading from her lips. "Is she feeling okay? She's going through a lot, right now."

Those words only upped his guilt level several notches. Marni was going through a lot. And instead of being a supportive friend Marni could lean on, he was toying with her emotions.

"She's fine, Nella," he quickly assured.

Nella leaned closer to her laptop. Even through the screen it was as if she could see clear to his soul.

"What is it? What aren't you telling me?" she demanded to know.

"Nothing. I mean, you're right. I should have asked her to come."

Nella's eyes narrowed on him, all too knowing. "Giovanni Santino. I swear if you've done anything to upset her."

"Listen, Nella. I have to go. My order's up." So what if he was fibbing. He hadn't actually ordered anything from anywhere. He just had to find a way off this call.

"Fine. But I'm not happy with you right now,

big bro. I'll call you later this evening. Both of you," she added in an ominous tone.

Gio ended the call and slipped the phone back into his pocket. Then he made a beeline for the furniture store. Whatever he had to do, that bed needed to be at the villa before tonight. He would hire the delivery van and find a driver if he had to.

Heck, if necessary, he would haul the bed back to the villa himself.

What do you want me to say?

How could he have asked her that? How could he not know?

Marni pounded the dough harder on the counter, trying to vent some of her frustration. Usually, the vigorous kneading and pounding calmed her nerves. Today it wasn't working so great toward that end.

The gall of that man. First to act like she had no business asking about his recovery. Then to kiss her so passionately that she'd actually felt her knees buckle.

And then the audacity of him to try and actually apologize for it.

Where was he, anyway? It had been hours since their little fiasco on the beach.

She'd already made the new bed—it had arrived a couple of hours after she'd gotten back to the villa following their eventful walk. Then she'd spent some time tidying and dusting. She'd even had a chance to watch another episode of her Bollywood show, which hadn't been nearly as enjoyable now that she was used to having company. Another mark against Gio Santino. He'd ruined her favorite pastime.

Now she was almost done with her kneading and he still wasn't back. She pounded the dough once more for good measure.

"Please tell me you're not picturing my face on that as you smack it that hard."

Startled, Marni whirled around to find Gio standing behind her in the doorway. She hadn't even heard him come in.

"Didn't mean to startle you," he added, walking farther into the kitchen.

Her irritation warred with the urge to run into his arms, and she silently berated herself. She could be such an idiot when it came to this man.

"What are you doing, anyway?"

"Making bread."

"I could have picked some up for you in town. You should have called and asked."

So that's where he'd been all this time. Marni pushed aside the dough and turned to face him, leaning her back against the counter. "And you could have called and told me where you were."

The corner of his mouth lifted. "Why? Were you worried about me?"

Of course she'd been worried. The man had a bad leg and other internal injuries he was just barely recovering from. But she wasn't about to take the bait.

"Of course not," she lied. "Just pointing out the polite thing to do when you're sharing a house with someone."

Gio visibly cringed. "You're the second person today to accuse me of being impolite. Which reminds me, Nella called earlier. Wants to talk to both of us later this evening."

Marni's eyebrows rose. "Is everything okay?"

He lifted his hand in reassurance. "She sounded fine. Just wanted to tell us both something. I was going to ask her more but our conversation got a little waylaid."

Huh. Curious.

What did he mean about a waylaid conversation with his sister? And what would Nella want to tell them both at the same time? So many questions and so few answers. Somehow, her life seemed so much more complicated during this trip when it was supposed to be a way for her to try and find some clarity about her future.

"The bed arrived," she told him, changing the topic. "I've already made it up with some fresh sheets I found in the linen closet."

Gio's response to that bit of news was surprisingly low-key. He merely nodded, then plucked a grape out of the fruit bowl and tossed it in his mouth. "Thanks. What else did you do today?"

So more small talk, then. So be it. She'd play along. For now. "I tidied, started this bread. And watched another episode of *Lotus Dream*."

Gio stopped chewing and swallowed, then tilted his head. "You…you watched an episode without me?" Marni almost felt a twinge of guilt at the dejection in his tone. Almost.

She shrugged. "Guess you'll have to catch up at some point."

"Guess so."

What do you want me to say?

His question from earlier echoed in her mind. So many words he might have come up with rather than asking it. Like, maybe he could have told her that he was just as confused as she was but not sorry about whatever it was happening between them. Or maybe tell her that he cared for her and always would, that they would figure things out together. He could have even told her that he'd enjoyed their kiss as much as she had, but needed time to process.

But Gio hadn't said any of those things. And he probably never would.

What did it matter at this point? In a few short days, she would be on her way back to the

States. She'd maybe see Gio four or five times a year when Nella invited her to various family functions. It would be as if this time spent together in Capri never happened.

Her eyes began to sting so she made a dramatic show of working the dough again, not that it needed it. In fact, if she pounded it any more at this point, the bread was sure to be a rubbery, chewy mess.

"Can I have some of that bread when it's done?" Gio asked, a charming, wide smile over his lips. "I'll trade you for some fresh fish I bought in town that I'm grilling for dinner."

She lifted her chin, not quite ready to accept any kind of olive branch. "I'll think about it."

Marni swam the length of the pool then lingered in the deep end just allowing herself to float. She let the warm water wash over her skin and soothe her tense muscles.

Why hadn't she done this before? A serene early evening swim to settle some of her frazzled nerves was exactly the ticket. The salty scent of the sea and the steady sound of the crashing waves in the distance added to the tranquility she'd so desperately needed.

With a relaxed sigh, she immersed herself fully in the water then held her breath for as long as she could. As if she could shut off the rest of the world, if only for the briefest of moments.

Finally popping up for air, she opened her eyes and gasped: Gio crouched by the edge of the pool. Honestly, he had to stop startling her like that. So much for relaxing, her pulse was rocketing again.

"You were under there quite awhile," he remarked. "I was about to jump in to get you."

Unbidden images flashed in her mind of the two of them frolicking in the pool together. Skin to skin. With complete privacy, unlike at the beach earlier.

She blinked the vision away. Her pulse now a rapid staccato.

"I was about to get dinner started," Gio informed her.

"That's fine. The bread should be done baking. I'll go get it." She swam over to the edge where Gio stood waiting for her. He'd grabbed her towel and was holding it out to her.

When she climbed out, Gio had the towel spread wide in his hands, waiting for her to step in it. Marni swallowed. Nothing to read in the gesture. The man was simply helping her dry off. She walked up to him and turned around, allowing him to drape the thick terry cloth over her shoulders. His hands lingered just long enough. She could feel the warmth of his palms through the fabric, the strength of his grasp. It took all her will not to move back closer against his chest and nestle herself against his length.

Instead, she savored the feel of his fingers on her shoulders. But it was over all too soon. He moved away and the chill of his loss immediately settled over her skin.

"I'll go get the coal grill fired up," he said behind her. "Take your time drying off."

She would need time. Not to dry off, but to quell the yearning in her core that must be written on her face. She could only do so much to hide her feelings for this man. It was exhausting her to try.

"Back in a few," she threw over her shoulder, before walking to the screen door and into the house.

When she returned a few minutes later dressed with her hair in a topknot, Gio was spooning the fish onto two plates. He'd poured them each a glass of wine. A sharp knife of sadness pierced through her heart at what might have been as she took in the sight. In a different life, they might have been a real couple about to enjoy a quiet evening enjoying each other's company, followed by a not so quiet night.

There she went again. Thinking in ways she had no business doing.

Taking a second to compose herself, Marni walked to the table and set the basket of bread in the center, next to the salad and antipasti.

"Fresh and hot," she announced with a casualness she didn't feel. She could only hope it wasn't the texture of gum given the way she'd punished the dough.

Gio pulled her chair out for her, then took the seat across the table. The fish was good, really good. Gio had kept it simple with just a couple of spices and a generous splash of lemon on each filet.

Why did the man have to be so good at everything he did? It was hard to stay angry at someone who'd made this great of a meal for you.

She was about to grudgingly compliment his cooking when he reached for the loaf and broke off the end piece then handed it to her wordlessly. The Santinos always gave Marni the end piece, it was the part she liked most.

When he went to bite his own slice, his eyes widened and his eyebrows furrowed. He chewed once. Then again. Then he stilled.

Marni took a bite and it confirmed her fears. The bread was chewy and dense. "Okay, so it's not my best work."

"I'll say. Not even a whole stick of butter would salvage this."

And he wasn't going to pull any punches.

"I'm sorry, Gio," she said, surprising herself as well as him given the way he set his fork down and focused on her face.

"Marni, you don't have to apologize for messing up bread. We have plenty else for dinner."

Marni put her fork down as well. "I guess that's not what I'm really apologizing for." Now that the words were out, she realized they needed to be said.

"Then what?" he asked gently.

"I think you know. I shouldn't have pushed you earlier today. You clearly don't want to talk about what you're doing to recover." *Or not doing*, she added silently. "It wasn't my place to pressure you about it."

Gio pushed his plate away. Great, now she could feel guilty that she'd ruined their appetites.

"Marni. You have to realize how important you are to us. To me, my sister, my mother. And my father before we lost him."

She swallowed. "I'd like to think I am. As important as the Santinos have always been to me."

"You remember how strict our parents were growing up. They were hard on both Nella and me."

She nodded. "I remember."

"You were the only one who stuck around,

put up with how rigid my parents' rules were. Nella would have no friends if it weren't for you."

The same could be said about her. Her mom was always at work and her dad had long ago left them. The Santinos were more family to her than anyone else.

Gio continued, his eyes imploring her to understand. "So you have to see why I can't break my sister's heart by having a meaningless fling with her best friend."

Ouch. He might as well have thrown the porcelain plate at her. Well, she'd be damned if she was going to let him see just how much he'd cut her with those words.

She plastered a forced smile on her face. "Of course. You're right, Gio. I completely agree."

Gio wanted to suck his words back in as soon as they left his mouth. He hadn't meant to sound quite so heartless. Just direct and unwavering. Damn. Why did he keep tripping up over himself when it came to Marni? He couldn't seem to stop messing things up with her.

She rose from the table before he could find a way to smooth over the edges of the words he'd used. "I'll take your plate if you're done," she offered, without so much as a glance at him.

Of course he was done. As if he could continue eating now. His delivery may have been shoddy, but surely she had to see the logic of what he'd been trying to say. Gio had nothing really to offer a woman right now, especially not one like Marni. For one thing, he was a wreck physically with nothing to look forward to but months, maybe years, of treatment and surgeries ahead of him. Some days he could hardly manage to walk without cringing in pain. He had no idea how he would juggle all that while manning the helm at Santino Foods.

Marni didn't wait for his answer about his plate. She took her own, grabbed the bread basket and walked into the house.

With a curse, Gio collected the remaining dishware off the table and joined her at the sink. They silently went about washing each piece as he scrambled his brain to think of something to say.

The sound of her phone ringing came from the other room. "That must be Nella," Marni said, shutting off the water and toweling her hands dry. She motioned for him to follow. "You said she wanted to talk to both of us."

For the first time in his life, Gio found himself grateful for a call from his chatty sister. Anything to distract from the tension between him and Marni right now.

He peered over her shoulder as she accepted

the video call. Nella's smiling face greeted them on the screen. Her husband, Alex, joined in the frame an instant later.

"Hello, you two," Nella said with a finger wave.

"Hi, Nella," Marni answered and a genuine smile lit up her face, her first one of the day that he could recall.

"Are you both sitting down?" she asked. "I think you need to sit down for this."

Marni cast a curious glance in Gio's direction. He shrugged in response. Damned if he had any clue or insight.

His sister's wide smile suggested that there was no need for alarm. But what exactly was she about to say that was so earth-shattering?

"Go sit," Nella insisted when they still hadn't moved.

Once they obliged, his sister actually squealed before speaking. "So, Alex and I have some big news to share with the two of you," she began.

To his surprise, Marni squealed just then too. "Oh, my God! Nella, really?" she asked.

Really what? What was all this about? Marni sounded as if she'd figured it out already. For the life of him he couldn't figure out how. Nella hadn't even said anything yet.

"Really, Marn," Nella said with a delighted laugh.

"That's wonderful!" Marni clasped a hand to her cheek.

"You and my brother are about to become godparents."

Godparents? But that would mean…

His sister confirmed before he could finish the thought. "I'm pregnant!"

Gio felt his jaw drop. His little sister. His *baby* sister was going to have a baby herself.

"Congratulations you two!" Marni exclaimed. "I'm so happy for you both."

Gio could only manage a nod and a feeble "Me too."

No one else seemed to notice just how dumbfounded he was. "We're only telling immediate family right now," Nella said, glancing up at her husband for confirmation. He gave it to her with a quick peck on her forehead.

His sister's eyes found his on the screen. "Well, what do you think, big bro?"

What he thought was that he was going to need some time to let the news sink in. Somehow, he found a better response for Nella's sake.

"I think you should be prepared for me to spoil this kid rotten. Right before I hand him back to you and take off."

Nella wagged a finger at him. "Or her. We don't know yet, Uncle Gio."

Uncle Gio. His new title. The phrase added another jolt to his already shocked system.

After several more minutes of happy chatter, Nella finally said her goodbyes and Marni exited the call, tossing her phone on the couch. Then she threw her arms around his neck and embraced him in a tight hug. Gio's arms reflexively went around her waist.

"I'm going to be an uncle," he said against her cheek, testing the words out himself, hardly able to believe they were coming out of his mouth.

Marni pulled back to beam him a dazzling smile. "And a godparent. Like me."

That's right. That was the other large piece in all this. He and Marni had yet one more major tie to each other. Nella's pregnancy was not about him of course, but he couldn't help but think it was yet another sign from the universe.

He couldn't play fast and loose with the woman he'd be sharing godparent duty with for the rest of his life.

CHAPTER TEN

MARNI STARED UP at the ceiling in her borrowed bedroom, still abuzz with the news. She was genuinely over the moon for her friend. Nella Santino deserved every bit of happiness. She was the purest, most genuine person Marni had ever met.

She and Alex were perfect for each other. Nella adored her new husband and the feeling was definitely mutual.

Nella's announcement certainly put things in perspective. Her friend had a fulfilling life with a doting, loving husband and she was about to be a mother. Whereas Marni's current relationship was completely made up for the sake of some media clicks. Speaking of which, she reached for her phone and scanned all the relevant websites. No photos of her and Gio, not yet, anyway. Clearly, their selfies weren't having much of an impact.

Marni sighed and turned over to her side,

her thoughts returning to her friend's big news. What must it be like to have found the love of your life? To be starting a family with him? Nella was lucky enough to have found her soul mate, and that couple in the Gardens of Augustus had looked so in love as well.

These days, Marni doubted such good fortune would ever be in the cards for her. Just look at her past romantic history. Albeit short, it included a man who'd mistreated her then ruined her career prospects. On the heels of that disaster, she'd somehow managed to fall in love with a man completely out of her reach.

Whoa.

Where had that come from?

Marni bolted upright. She had inadvertently wandered into dangerous territory. Gio Santino had been her crush for years, she rationalized. Her attraction to him was simply at the forefront of her mind now because of their proximity and the romantic setting. She couldn't go believing she'd somehow really fallen in love with the man.

Or maybe you've always been in love with him.

Marni rubbed her eyes, squeezing them shut under her fingers. She needed some air. Despite the late hour, she threw on a thin sweater and made her way downstairs.

The light on the patio was already on when she reached the first floor. Gio was out there, sitting by the pool. She debated turning right around, heading back to the room, but too late, his head snapped up and he gave her a small wave.

With a resigned sigh, Marni went over to the screen door and stepped outside. Silver moonlight bathed the patio and beach in the distance. Bright stars dotted the dark sky like diamonds on dark velvet. If she had to paint a picture of the perfect setting for a romantic interlude, this was exactly what she might put to canvas. Complete with the man of her fantasies sitting front and center.

"My insomnia must be catching," Gio told her once she reached his side.

"I'm too excited for Nella to sleep." That was close enough to the truth. "What about you," she asked, "Don't tell me the new bed isn't comfortable."

He shook his head. "It's perfect. Definitely beats the lounge chair."

"So why are you out here on said chair instead of upstairs in the comfortable bed?"

"Thought I could use the air."

"Hmm."

"You didn't seem all that surprised, about Nella expecting."

Marni shrugged. "I saw how in love she and Alex are with each other. I know family has always been a big part of your sister's life. I guess I just saw it coming sooner or later."

"Well, it was much sooner than I would have expected. Not that I'd given it much thought."

Marni wasn't surprised. Men could be so unaware sometimes. Even about those closest to them. "You'll get used to the idea."

Gio scoffed. "It's still sinking in. Though there might be an advantage for me here with this new development."

"Yeah? How so?"

"Maybe Mama will go easier on the pestering for me to settle down and start a family."

The thought of Gio with a wife, sharing children with some to-be-determined woman, had Marni's stomach clenching in knots. She could just picture him with a doe-eyed, dark-haired beauty as they held hands with their little ones. Maybe she'd be one of the models or actresses he'd been linked to in the past, not that it was any of her business. Marni pushed the image aside.

She was not in love with him! All the pretending was warping her perception of reality.

"She must be over the moon," she said. Signora Santino might have been strict and demanding, but she'd always been one to show deep affection. Marni couldn't think of anyone more fitting for the Italian grandmother role. Straight out of central casting.

Gio shifted his chair to turn and face her. "Listen, Marni. I think this is a good time to get some things straight. I don't want things to be strained between us."

Uh-oh. Marni was afraid to guess where this was leading.

"Especially now," Gio continued. "We're going to be godparents together. Nella's going to need us both to be there for her. And her child is going to need us for the rest of his or her life."

Nothing to argue with there.

"Let's do what we need to, to put whatever started this rift between us in the trash bin. Forget it ever happened."

He meant their kiss. He wanted to pretend he'd never kissed her. Would it be so easy for him to do as he was suggesting? To just wipe from his mind that he'd been shaking with need while he'd held her in his arms with his lips on hers?

What a fool she was. That one kiss had changed everything for her. She went to bed thinking about it at night and woke up with it on her mind the next morning.

"I think that would be for the best," she answered, even as her heart ached in her chest.

He stood suddenly. "Stay put, I'll be right back."

"Where are you going?"

"Since neither of us can sleep, I say we do some celebrating. I thought I saw some nice champagne in the cellar when I first got here. If you're up for it. I know it's rather late."

She was indeed up for it, Marni decided. After all, it wasn't like she was going to get to sleep anytime soon. "Sure," she answered. "Why not? Let's toast to Nella's news."

He flashed her a dazzling smile. "And we can toast to our newfound understanding too."

Two days later Gio entered the house with a fresh box of pastries, rather pleased with himself. He'd gotten to the bakery stand early enough to get all of Marni's favorites. More importantly, since their little chat on the patio the other night, things between them felt pretty much back to normal. It helped that they had a common interest and desire to talk all the ways they planned on spoiling his niece or nephew.

Well, things were mostly normal, if he didn't count all those times he caught himself noticing the fullness of Marni's lips after she applied her favorite lip balm. Or how her hair became curlier from seaside humidity after she spent time on the beach. Or how her skin was growing more golden with each passing day, leading him to wonder about what tan lines she might have underneath her clothes.

Six days. She'd be leaving in six days. He only needed to hold it together for that long. The thought should have been a comforting one. But the idea of being here at this villa without her didn't exactly hold the appeal it should have. There'd be no one to share pastries with, to grill fish for. To spend sleepless nights with on the patio sipping on champagne or iced tea.

Gio was about to set the box down and transfer the goodies onto a serving plate when a loud thud sounded from upstairs. The sound was followed by a harsh feminine cry. Marni. Something was wrong. Gio tossed the box onto the counter then ran for the stairs and jogged up them to her room, ignoring the bolt of pain that shot through his muscles at the effort.

He found her door open and Marni sitting on the bed. Her hands were clenched at her sides, her cheeks red with a look of horror on her face.

"What's wrong?"

She swallowed, tears welling up in her eyes, and pointed to the floor. Gio followed her finger to where her tablet lay screen down on the carpet.

"That rat!" Marni cried, her voice full of anguish. For a split second, Gio thought maybe she was speaking literally. Had a rodent gotten in the house? But Marni didn't look scared, she looked angry. And panicked.

So a figurative rat then.

Gio bent down and reached for the device. The page Marni must have been reading was still up on the screen. He scanned it just enough to see what Marni was so worked up about. She had every right. In fact, his own blood pressure had skyrocketed as he read the words.

"Why the son of a—"

Marni stood and began pacing the room. "He's making up all sorts of lies about me."

Gio scanned more of the article. It was a piece in a trade mag. Ander Stolis was the featured subject. "Your ex is quite a piece of work."

Marni slammed a fist on the bureau, enough to make her toiletries jump. "He says he was particularly stressed working on his latest designs because of a young colleague who was obsessed with him. That she practically stalked him after he broke things off with her." She laughed bitterly. "What complete bull." She pointed to her chest. "Everyone knows who he means. Me!"

"Marni, you can send out a statement." He held the tablet up. "Email this editor. Tell him this is all a load of crock. You can set the record straight."

"How?" she demanded, her eyes blazing with fury and shiny wet with unshed tears. "It's his word against mine. And he has much more clout in that world than I do."

Gio clenched his fists tight. If the lowlife were standing in front of him right now, Gio had all sorts of ideas about what he might do. All of it too good for the likes of such a liar.

He knew for a fact none of the claims quoted in the piece were even remotely true. How in the world would Marni be pleading with Ander to get back together? For one, she'd been with *him* almost constantly since she'd arrived on the island.

"He says I sent him countless emails and messages and called repeatedly, begging him to take me back. All conveniently erased I might add. Because he wanted to erase all reminders of me as it was too upsetting and interfering with his work."

"People will have to see how suspect that is."

"Some might. Plenty of others won't. Ander has all the advantage here. I'll have no hope of finding another design position. Most definitely not in Boston. And probably not even in New York now. Not after all these accusations.

He makes me sound downright unstable. Who would take a risk on hiring someone like that?"

"This is complete character assassination. He can't get away with it."

Her response to that was to throw her head back and release a guttural groan full of frustration and misery. "So much for our playacting. It's being completely ignored. No one seems to care."

Gio reached for her, pulled her against him, began rubbing her upper arms. "I guess we'll just have to be more convincing. Our initial attempts at getting our pictures out there clearly haven't been impactful enough. We need to do more."

She leaned back to meet his eyes. The tightness around her mouth loosened ever so slightly. "What does that mean?"

He shrugged. "Clearly, we need to be more high profile about our romance."

Marni wasn't sure she liked the sound of this. What exactly did Gio mean by higher profile? "I'm not really following, Gio."

"Think about it. This Arfin, or whatever his name is—"

"Ander," she corrected, though she could think of plenty other choice words to call the man.

Gio waved his hand dismissively. "Whatever.

He's claiming you're still hung up on him. That you've made his life miserable because you can't stand that he's dumped you. We need to be more convincing. And more visible."

"I'm listening," she prompted.

"No more staged photos and appearances in the hope that we might get noticed."

"And we do what instead exactly?" she asked, her eyes still shiny with anger.

"We go to places and events that are sure to be covered. A place where there's sure to be VIPs."

She nodded. "Celebrities and famous people."

"Exactly. Capri is practically a celebrity magnet. And where there's celebrities…" He motioned for her to complete the sentence.

"There's paparazzi."

"Bingo. Then it's just a matter of my social media people sending anonymous notes to various magazines and sites. With the photos to round out the story."

Marni could only nod, trying to fully process all that he was saying.

Gio continued, "Far from a jilted ex who can't let go, you'll be shown as a happy, fulfilled woman who's moved on and found real love. And I'll be able to further redirect any media attention about me to my newfound relationship, as opposed to my near fatal accident. Love conquers all, as they say."

Good thing Marni wasn't drinking or eating anything at the moment. The way Gio kept saying "love" while referring to the two of them would have no doubt made her choke.

"Plus, there's an event we can attend. One with guaranteed cameras present."

"What kind of event?" she asked, focusing on the bare logistics of this plan of his.

"It so happens Santino Foods has an event in Naples in a couple of days."

"I'm listening."

"Every year, we host a charity gala to raise money and awareness for displaced children of wars and global conflict."

"I remember hearing and reading about it. Santino does a lot for worthy causes." Like the one that had led him to personally race in a rally.

He nodded. "Like most years, it's being held at the exclusive Grande Napolitano Hotel and Resort. Black tie, formal, live entertainment. There's always plenty of press there."

"You never mentioned a gala."

He shrugged. "I wasn't planning on going but I'll tell them I've changed my mind."

"You weren't going to go to your own annual event? You're the CEO."

He sighed wearily, rubbed a hand down his affected leg. "People understood why when I sent my regrets. I have plenty of high-level managers and PR people who don't need me there."

Marni let that knowledge sink in. Something fluttered in her chest. Gio had no intention of going to a major company event. He was too bruised and battered to be there. But he was going now. For her.

"I don't know what to say," she told him. The day so far had been a roller coaster of emotion. Waking up to that awful article and all those terrible lies about her had felt like a wrecking ball to her midsection. Now she felt touched and grateful at all that Gio was willing to do to help her make it all go away. "Except to tell you thank you…for being willing to do all this."

He nodded once. "I'm doing it for my sake too. And for Juno's."

Maybe, Marni thought. But she wasn't naive. Gio could have probably found a much easier way to garner some publicity than a sham relationship. No, the pretending was mostly for her benefit.

She looked up to find his hand waving in front of her face. "Marni? Where did you just drift off to?"

"I was just thinking whether we can pull this off."

He cast a smile her way that had her insides quivering. "Of course we can. I know just where to start tomorrow night."

"Where?"

"There's a nightclub in town. Owned and run by a trained musician. Every weekend night he plays live music with a full band. At least one or two international celebrities are bound to show up."

"Which means cameras and picture taking."

He winked at her. "You got it. We can go tomorrow night. Make it a night on the town."

"Gio, I don't know. For one thing, are you up for it? You were in so much pain after the grotto."

His eyes narrowed on her, and a dark shadow passed over his face. "Don't worry about me, gattina. I can handle it."

Great. She'd offended him. She was about to tell him that acknowledging his injury was nothing to be insulted by. Did Gio honestly think himself lesser because of his injuries? Before she could get a word in, he thrust the tablet toward her until she took it.

"The only question is what will you decide to do," he told her, his voice challenging. "Are you going to push back and defend yourself? Or are you going to let him continue to get away with taunting you?"

With that, he turned away and left the room, shutting the door firmly behind him. Marni heard a slew of Italian words and curses as he descended the stairs.

Marni flopped backward onto the bed and swiped the slanderous article off the screen. Then she deleted the entire app for good measure.

No. She certainly wasn't going to let Ander Stolis get away with repeatedly smearing her name.

She *would* push back. She *would* defend herself.

Her friend was positively glowing. Even through her computer monitor Marni could see plainly how radiant and happy Nella appeared.

"You look great, Nella. Pregnancy definitely agrees with you."

Nella flashed her a wide smile. "Thanks, Marn. It may appear so, this time of day anyhow."

Concern flushed through Marni's core. "What do you mean? Are you not feeling well?"

Nella placed her palm above her rib cage. "The morning sickness is kind of kicking my behind. Takes me a good two hours to get past the queasiness and get out of bed."

Oh, no. Nella had always been a morning person. Being hampered the first part of her day had to be difficult for someone like her.

"I could use some of your vanilla pancakes. Been craving those," Nella told her.

"As soon as I'm back, I'm going to make them for you every morning."

"Thanks." Nella wagged a finger at her. "But don't even think about coming back early on account of me. You promised me you'd take it easy for the full two weeks."

If Nella only knew. This vacation had been less "take it easy" and more "what curve ball is next?"

"Don't you dare renege," Nella added.

"I won't. Promise."

"Good. Besides, Alex is trying his hand at those pancakes and he's getting better every day."

The twist of Nella's lips indicated that Alex might still have a way to go. How sweet of him to try for his wife. A wave of sadness rose in her chest. She couldn't recall any time a man she'd been involved with had tried to make her breakfast.

Though Gio made sure to keep the breakfast pastries in full supply. Hardly the same thing. Still…

"So, what's new?" Nella wanted to know,

pulling her out of her thoughts. "You just calling to check on me and the bambino?"

Primarily. "Of course."

"And?"

"I just wanted to tell you that if you see anything online, about Gio and me, that it's not real. We're just trying to put on a show. I'll explain more later. You have enough going on right now."

Nella tilted her head. "Okay…"

She had to laugh at her expression.

"What else?" Nella asked.

Her friend could always read her so well. Marni wasn't surprised she'd picked up on the fact that there were more than a couple reasons for this call.

"Actually, there is one more thing," Marni began. "I also had a question."

"Shoot."

"I was wondering where you went in town to get your hair done. And where you'd shop if you needed a new dress."

CHAPTER ELEVEN

Soon after hanging up with Nella, Marni walked the mile and a half down the beach to the water taxi station her friend had informed her about. Gio was deep in emails on his laptop, so she'd simply left him a note.

She did some mentally calculations taking into account her bank balance, upcoming expenses and the exchange rate. Depending on how much the beauty salon was going to charge, she would no doubt have to skimp on the dress. One thing was certain, there was no way Marni could afford the upscale boutique Nella had suggested. She'd have to make do and find something relatively inexpensive.

A text popped up on her phone screen while she waited for the taxi boat. It was as if Nella was reading her mind.

Tell Gio to charge the salon and dress to a company expense account. You're attending a corporate function so it checks.

Marni smiled with appreciation but there was no way she was going to take the Santinos up on that. She wouldn't type that to Nella, however. Or she'd end up having to ditch the other woman's calls all day. She sent the heart emoji instead.

The floating dots appeared immediately on the screen.

You're not going to do it, are you?

Of course she wasn't. This time Marni sent a smiley face.

When she reached town twenty minutes later, the salon was only a brief walk away.

Using the translation app on her phone, along with the rudimentary Italian she'd learned spending so much time with the Santinos, Marni explained what she was after.

The stylist, a stunning brunette with bright red lips and dark wavy hair, gave her a dubious look.

"Sei sicuro?" the other woman asked.

Marni nodded. *"Sì."* Yes, she was sure.

She'd given this a lot of thought. No matter what happened with this little facade of theirs, Marni planned to go into it as a different person. She would start with her looks. She couldn't remember the last time she'd altered her appearance. Marni was due.

The woman who'd allowed Ander to control and belittle her, with hardly a word in her defense, was gone for good. Never to return. She was different now.

Marni was going to make sure to look the part.

Something on her face must have convinced the stylist, because she grinned and got to work. Marni spent the better part of the afternoon in the chair. When she was finally done three and a half hours later—transforming yourself was a long process—she nearly squealed in delight at the results.

The stylist was a genius. She'd taken what Marni had said and expanded on it. The result was a stunning and modern hairstyle that brought out the shape of her face. If she did say so herself. Despite her measly bank account, she gave the woman a generous tip. The stylist had earned every penny.

Let's see Gio make fun of her ponytail now... She stopped herself mid thought. No. These changes were for her and her alone. Gio's reaction was sure to be just a bonus.

So why did her heart pound with nervous anticipation at the thought of what he might say about her new hair?

Marni would find out soon enough. Right now, she had to move on to the next phase of her trip into town. The dress.

Even looking at the window display of the boutique Nella had recommended was enough to confirm what she already knew. Her credit card might not have been declined, but it would take Marni a good long time to pay it off.

It didn't help that everyone around here was impeccably dressed in the latest styles. Her simple beige wraparound dress fell far short. Particularly compared to the young lady Marni eyed sitting alone sipping a coffee at the café next door to the shop.

Marni shoved away her shyness and walked over to the woman. What did she have to lose?

"Scusa," she began, approaching the woman's table. "Er... *Dove posso trovare."* She indicated the woman's outfit with her hand.

With a warm, friendly smile, the woman gestured for Marni's phone. When she handed it back, a name and address had been typed on the screen.

"Un piccolo negozio. Poco costoso," the woman said, pointing across the piazza to a side street.

Marni wanted to hug the other woman with appreciation. *A small store. Not too expensive.* Exactly what she was looking for.

The next time she saw herself in the mirror of a small dressing room, Marni had to pinch herself to confirm it was really her in the glass.

The new her.

Gio heard the door shut from the first-floor study and finished off his email then hit Send. Finally. Marni had been gone most of the day. With nothing but a note informing him she'd gone into town.

Why hadn't she asked him to take her?

They could have had lunch together. Done some sightseeing. Plus, they needed to talk about their exact plans for this evening. Shouldn't they discuss how they wanted to act? The image they wanted to project to the world?

Gio knew tonight would be all for show. But he wanted it to go smoothly. For Marni's sake.

Right. As if that was the only reason. It had been so long since he'd been out with a woman, and he'd never had to do so while in pain before. What if Marni had been right to ask about his readiness. What was he going to do if the pain became too much? It wasn't as if he could find a bag of ice or elevate his foot as he fought the waves of agony. Could he keep the pain at bay for a few hours given the stakes?

Well, before the night was over, he'd find out one way or another.

By the time he rose and went out to the sitting room, she had already dashed upstairs. A moment later, he heard her voice echoing from above. She must have called Nella.

Great. Marni had been gone all day and now she was holed up in her room talking to his sister, a conversation that could very well take over an hour. Those two always spent forever talking to each other once they got started. And now that Nella was pregnant, there was a litany of baby topics they could chat about.

Gio swore and went back to his laptop. His mood had been sour all day, now it was downright acidic. He couldn't even explain why.

He didn't need to spend every day with Marni. They'd be together all evening, after all. It wasn't as if he'd missed her while she was gone.

Gio adjusted his tie and glanced at his watch, a ritual he must have completed at least a half dozen times in the last hour. He and Marni would have to leave in a few minutes if they wanted to make any kind of noticeable entrance.

He debated icing his leg yet again but decided against it. It was on the brink of frostbite as it was.

Instead, he loosened the knot of his tie for the umpteenth time. He was out of practice as far as wearing one. The last time he'd gone out in a suit was before the accident. He'd been a completely different person then. His highest priority had been the next growth opportunity for Santino Foods and his main concern the latest sales figures and profit margins.

He still paid attention to those things, of course. Gio still made sure to monitor the industry, kept up with the distributors and read up on all the newest, trendiest Italian restaurants in major cities across the world. But numbers on a spreadsheet seemed much less life-and-death now. He supposed his turnabout was hardly surprising, given that he'd survived an actual literal life-and-death scenario.

What was taking Marni so long? He'd heard the shower shut off a good forty-five minutes ago. Was she stalling? Losing her nerve to go through with this?

After about ten more minutes of waiting, Gio made the decision to go check on her ETA. The turn of her doorknob sounded just as he reached the first step and he sighed in relief. He hadn't realized until that moment how nervous he'd been that she'd changed her mind about tonight. Which made no sense whatsoever. It wasn't as if he was looking forward to being gawked at on his first night out since the accident.

And then Marni descended the stairs and he lost all ability to think at all.

"I'm ready to go," she announced but he could hardly hear over the pounding in his ears.

Marni was…different. Her hair was cut and set in a completely different style with subtle bronze highlights throughout. It fell around her face in soft willowy strands, the ends reaching just above her shoulders. The waves were no more, replaced by a straightened thick mane that glittered where the light hit it.

He cleared his throat, finally managed to summon some words. "You, uh, got your hair cut."

Her hand reached up and she ran a finger through the fringe of her bangs, also new. "A good four inches. What do you think?"

What he thought was how much he wanted to be the one running his hands through those tresses. Of course, he wasn't about to actually say that. Trouble was, he couldn't come up with anything *to* say.

Marni's eyes widened with what looked like alarm. "You don't like it? Is it too drastic a change?"

Oh, no. He couldn't have her go thinking he didn't like it. He did. He liked it very, very much.

Then there was the dress. Gio ran his gaze down the length of her. Whisper-thin straps sat over golden tanned shoulders. The navy silky number draped over her curves in all the right ways, the skirt coming to a stop right above her knees. Her legs were bare but, heaven help him, did they have some kind of glittery powder on them? He didn't even know that was a thing. Strappy dark blue high heels adorned her feet. The pink polish was gone, replaced by a scarlet red that reminded him of the finest Toscana Rossa.

"Gio," she asked, "what do you think?" She gestured toward her midsection. "Will this do for tonight?"

Somehow, he kept himself from yelling outright that Yes! it would more than do. The only problem with it was how much he wanted to slip the dress off her and then proceed to muss up her stylish hair in all manner of ways.

Marni pointed to her head. "Is it the hair? Or the dress?"

That had him dumbstruck. It was the whole package. Where had all this come from? Where had this Marni come from? Gone was the familiar, conservatively dressed prim and proper gattina he'd grown up with. In her place stood a strikingly stunning woman who could easily fit walking down a runway or featured in a magazine fashion spread.

Marni had always been pretty. But now she was absolutely beautiful.

He had to stop gawking somehow and find something to say.

When he met Marni's gaze again she was staring at him, her lips tight with apprehension.

"Should I change?" she asked. "Or wash out my hair to bring the curls back?" She searched his face. "Both? Should I change all of it?"

The question had him snapping out of his stupor. "Don't even think about it, Marni," he finally managed. His voice sounded thick and strained to his own ears. "Don't you dare change a thing."

She felt like a princess on her way to the royal ball. Her companion certainly fit the image of the handsome prince. Of course, she'd seen Gio dressed up in the past. Prom night came to mind, and various formal functions she'd attended as a guest of the Santino family. But never before had she been the one on his arm.

The thought made her light-headed. She stole a glance at him now as they made their way into the club. In a dark navy suit Marni was certain was custom-tailored, Gio looked polished and devilishly handsome. A light gray shirt topped with a silk tie rounded out the image. He looked every bit the successful, coveted bachelor that he was. How unexpected that she was the woman he'd be spending the evening with.

Steady there, girl. This is all just for show, don't forget.

Still, she couldn't help but think of the way Gio had stared at her as she made her way down the stairs, and the memory sent feminine pleasure surging through her chest. He'd truly appreciated her new look. No doubt, her ex would have found a way to put down her makeover. Or even mock her for trying something different with her appearance.

Marni gave her head a shake. No more thoughts about Ander tonight. He wasn't worth it.

The band wasn't onstage yet but already the place was packed. Not one empty table. She wondered how Gio had snagged the last one.

The place was decorated to look like an ancient roman castle. A large mural painting of the Parthenon covered one wall.

Marni scanned the others in attendance: definitely an A-list crowd. Subconsciously, she fingered the costume jewelry earring on her earlobe. The other women in here were decked out in high-karat diamonds and other precious stones.

Who did she think she was fooling?

The better question was whether she was only fooling herself thinking she could fit into a place like this, with her bargain dress and faux leather shoes.

Gio must have sensed her self-doubt, maybe her expression had given him a clue. "You look beautiful, Marni. Absolutely beautiful," he said. A darkness settled over his eyes that left her insides quivering. His compliment served as a boost to her wavering confidence, and Marni suspected that was exactly what Gio had intended.

"Thanks, Santino. You clean up pretty nice yourself."

"Good thing. Because I haven't worn a suit in ages and I feel like I'm wrapped like an Egyptian mummy." Gio stuck his finger in his collar and made a choking sound.

He was trying to get a laugh out of her, must have sensed how nervous she was. Marni reached for his other hand on the table. "Thank you, Gio. For doing all this." She meant it. He was uncomfortable and achy, out on the town when he should be home resting his bruised and battered body. For her.

Gio's hand clenched under hers. "You can thank me by trying to relax and have a good time. Just because we're here on a mission doesn't mean we can't enjoy it."

"I'll try." She knew she should pull her hand away right then but let it linger, skin against skin. Finally, she pulled her arm back to her side when their server arrived.

Marni understood enough of the language to know that Gio ordered the night's special cocktail for them both and a bottle of champagne to share, along with an antipasto tray. Within moments of getting their food and drinks, the band appeared onstage and took their seats.

Soon the sound of traditional Neapolitan music filled the air. Before the end of the first song, several couples had already moved onto the dance floor.

Gio leaned over to speak in her ear. "Do you recognize the young lady in the leopard print dress?" he asked her.

Marni zoned in on the subject of his question. A petite blonde in impossibly high stilettos. She definitely looked familiar. It dawned on her why in a few seconds. "She's the latest addition to the cast of those superhero movies."

Gio nodded. "That's right. I'm certain at least a dozen people are snapping pictures of her right now. Pictures that will find themselves onto various gossip sites by morning."

Marni scanned the crowd. He certainly wasn't wrong. Several cell phones were held in the young actress's general direction.

"So if we want to be in any of those pictures, and hence on the websites, we should go up there now."

Marni swiveled her head and blinked at him. Was he suggesting that they actually join her on the dance floor? What about his hurt leg?

Before she could figure out how to ask without offending him again, Gio had stood up and was holding his hand out to her.

"Dance with me, gattina."

Marni's heart jumped in her chest. Silly as it might have been, it had never occurred to her that they'd be dancing together at some point tonight. Gio remained standing with his hand extended. He tilted his head questioningly when she still didn't rise out of her seat.

She swallowed, shoved her doubts away and stood, taking his hand. Gio's shoulders dropped with relief. He led her onto the dance floor. And then she was in his arms, her cheek against his shoulder, his arms around her waist.

The song was a soulful melody. She may not have understood all the lyrics but she knew the tempo of a love song when she heard it. Reflexively, she nestled closer against Gio's frame, allowed herself a deep inhalation of his aftershave.

Gio rubbed his cheek against the top of her head. Being in his arms again felt like being home. She hadn't even realized how badly she'd wanted to be there.

The song ended but Gio didn't let her go. Instead, he lifted her chin with his finger, then placed the gentlest of kisses on her lips. Marni's heart stopped, a jolt of electricity shot through her core. She wanted to ask him to do it again. But for longer this time, so that she could once again savor the taste of him. The way she had on the beach that day.

A small flash of light shone in the corner of her eye.

"There it is," Gio said with a satisfied tone and it hit her then: someone had snapped a photo. That was the whole reason he'd been kissing her in the first place. Shame and embarrassment had heat rushing to her face. When would she learn? It served her right. A reminder of why they were here. How could she have forgotten for even a moment that all of this was meant for the photos?

None of it was real.

He was in no mood.

Nella had picked the wrong time to tease him. He wasn't even going to bother replying to her text. She may be pregnant, but she was still the pesky little sister who knew exactly how to get under his skin.

Saw the pictures from last night online. You and Marni make quite a striking couple.

That part wasn't so bad. It was the kissy face emojis, at least a dozen of them, that she'd stuck on at the end that rankled his nerves. Nella knew why he and Marni had been out last night. She'd even called yesterday to tell him he was a sweetie and a *tesoro* for helping Marni to thwart her ex's toxic campaign against her.

What Nella didn't know, nor Marni for that matter, was just how real it had all felt in the moment. On the dance floor, he'd simply meant to pose for a picture when he'd planted that kiss on Marni's lips. Just another way to continue the facade. But something had shifted in his center when he'd had his lips on hers. Their momentary loss of control on the beach had been full of emotion, with tensions running high for them both.

In contrast, the kiss last night had felt tender, delicate. Yet all the more powerful somehow. It had shaken him to the core the way he'd wanted to take her mouth again. Right there on the dance floor. He hadn't even cared that they were in a crowded nightclub, surrounded by strangers. And he no longer cared about getting some silly photo to send to a magazine.

She appeared in the doorway a moment later.

Gio did a double take when he saw her, still not quite used to her new look. Short hair suited her. He hoped she kept it that length.

What was wrong with him?

The way Marni wore her hair was none of his business. And he had no business wallowing about a chaste little kiss they'd shared in the middle of a dance floor.

"Anything yet?" She pointed to his phone.

Gio shook his head. "Yes and no. It's just hitting the mainstream sites now. It'll take a couple more days before people figure out who you are and it gets to the trade mags."

She pushed her bangs off her forehead and blew out a frustrated breath. "It stinks that we have to do this. I wish there was some other way."

Did she mean having to go out with him? He thought she'd had fun last night. Enjoyed his company.

Last night was the most fun he'd had since the accident. Maybe even before it. Despite the way his leg and torso had screamed all night at the punishment of dancing.

He ignored the lump of disappointment that seemed to have formed in his gut. "We'll just have to get through the launch party tonight. Hopefully it will generate more publicity and attention."

She blew out a breath. "I really hope so. Then we can be done with this farce once and for all."

Gio flinched where he stood, hoping Marni didn't notice.

CHAPTER TWELVE

MARNI RAN THE brush through her hair one last time and adjusted the scarf around her neck. Last night had been magical. Until she'd realized that like most magic, it was all smoke and mirrors. All the joy and thrill she'd experienced burst like a needle-pricked balloon in that moment. Then she'd just wanted it to be over.

At least she was more mentally prepared this time. She wouldn't allow herself to get carried away like a schoolgirl if Gio kissed her again. Or fake-kissed her, that was.

When she made it downstairs, Gio was dressed and waiting. He offered her a rather weak smile that didn't quite seem genuine.

"Ready to go?" he asked. Unlike last night, he didn't offer her his arm this time.

"As I'll ever be. The sooner we get there, the sooner we get this over with."

He gave her a curt nod and led her out the door.

Hard to believe but he looked even more dashingly handsome than he had at the club. Tonight he wore a tux that matched the black of his hair. He'd used some kind of gel to keep it in place, whereas yesterday it fell in waves over his forehead. If the man ever got tired of this business tycoon thing, he definitely had a future as a men's cologne model.

She, for one, would be ready to buy anything Gio Santino was selling.

A speedboat with a uniformed skipper awaited them when they reached the beach. Gio helped her onboard and led her to a comfortable seating area below deck with a circular table larger than the one she had in her apartment. A tray of fresh fruit and a variety of cheeses sat in the center, along with an airing bottle of wine and two stem glasses.

Gio poured them each a glass but she only took a sip, guzzling from the frosty water bottle instead. Best to try and keep her wits about her for as long as she could manage.

"I've never been to Naples before," she said by way of conversation. Gio was being oddly quiet. She wished he would tell her more about what to expect. The last Santino function she'd been to was a corporate Christmas party when she was seventeen in the North End, Boston's equivalent of Little Italy. This one tonight would actually be in Italy.

The motor roared to life and soon they were making their way across the ocean, the craft accelerating gradually until they reached a speed that had the scenery outside the windows zipping by.

For the second time in two nights, Marni wondered if she was going to be underdressed. Maybe she should have saved last night's dress for this evening instead, it was just a tad fancier. But last night, she'd been concerned about impressing Gio. Such a wasted effort on her part.

She checked her reflection in a side panel mirror. And thought she heard Gio snort.

Her eyes snapped on his face to find him looking at her with pursed lips and darkened eyes. "Something wrong?"

"You seem overly concerned again about your appearance. I told you yesterday you looked beautiful. How many compliments are you fishing for?"

Marni felt her jaw drop and her chest stung with a sudden flash of anger. "What?"

Gio rubbed his jaw. "Never mind. Forget I said anything. You look great, okay? Stop worrying about it."

Well, he'd seen to that. Now all she'd be worried about was why he was being so surly and offensive. Clearly, he didn't want to be here on this boat on his way to a function he'd had no intention of attending if it hadn't been for her. None of that was her fault, damn it.

"May I remind you that all this was your idea?"

His eyes bore into hers and he shook his head. "No, you don't need to remind me. And I'm sorry it's so taxing for you to go through with it."

Marni sucked in a breath. Where was all this coming from? "I never said that."

"You didn't exactly have to spell it out."

The chime of an incoming text interrupted her reply. From Nella.

Too bad it can't be real.

She'd attached a well-known meme of a disappointed cartoon character. Marni squinted at her screen. What exactly was that supposed to mean? Damned if she could guess. Honestly, the Santino siblings were insistent on testing her nerves tonight.

She was about to text her back to ask for some clarity when Gio spoke. "We're here." He then stood, adjusting his gold cuff links.

Marni was surprised to look out the window and see the spectacular sight of Naples. Bright lights reflected off the water and lit up the clear night sky. She might have been looking at colorful fireworks somehow suspended in the air. The scene took her breath away. She imagined this was what Mount Olympus might look like.

Marni couldn't help but gawk at the sight as Gio led her off the boat and into a waiting limousine.

Less than ten minutes later, they arrived at the circular driveway of a sprawling resort. Marni could have sworn she'd seen this exact hotel in a spy movie not too long ago. Definitely worth an internet search to confirm as soon as she got a chance.

They walked down the brightly lit hallway toward the open double doors of a ballroom. The party appeared to be in full swing already.

Gio guided her through the entry with his hand at the small of her back. Marni forced herself not to react to his touch.

Even now, when she was furious with his behavior and at a complete loss to guess what might have caused it, she felt a current of electricity travel from the palm of his hand, clear through her skin and up the length of her spine.

The room seemed to still as they entered, the noise level decreased several decibels. Many heads turned in their direction at once. Marni supposed it made sense, the CEO had just arrived, after all. But there was something else she sensed in the air, a wave of curiosity.

She heard Gio utter a curse in Italian under his breath.

On instinct, she reached for his hand and gripped it tight behind her back. He squeezed back.

"Let's get a drink."

"All right." Sounded good to her; she was beginning to regret turning down the wine on the boat. Being the subject of such widespread scrutiny was not a comfortable feeling, nor one she was used to.

"I'm afraid we're going to have to mingle," Gio told her after he'd ordered them a couple of cocktails.

Sure. She could do that. All she had to do was smile and nod, right? Gio was the main attraction here, not her.

He looked less than pleased about it.

But he didn't falter. No less than half a dozen people approached him as they waited for their drinks. A couple simply wanted to say hello. The rest had urgent grievances and important matters and weren't going to waste this opportunity to bend the boss's ear.

Gio listened patiently, offered solutions or provided follow-up guidance. He really knew his stuff and was good at what he did.

Not that she'd ever doubted it.

Still, it was something else to see him in action. No wonder the company had grown several-fold under his guidance. Santino Foods was lucky to have him.

It was after they'd gotten their drinks and were headed toward their reserved table that the world shifted. Marni felt a splash of ice-cold liquid over her arm and middle. A heavy weight pushed against her side, followed by a hard thud by her feet. Marni's heart stopped as she processed what was happening: Gio had lost his balance. In horror, she looked down to find him braced on one knee gripping the base of a nearby table to keep from, going all the way down. His face a tight mask of agony.

"Oh, my God! Gio! Are you okay?" She dropped down next to him, reached for his arms. "Here, let me help you up."

The look he gave her had her breath catching in her throat. Red-hot anger burned behind his eyes. His voice was low and thick when he spoke. There was no mistaking the fury behind his words as he bit them out through tightly gritted teeth. "Marni. Don't."

Never in his worst nightmares had Gio imagined the scenario he found himself in. A room full of his colleagues and his employees, all present to see his horror. Then there was Marni. She'd had a front-row seat to it all.

His leg had actually given out, refused to support him. It had happened in a split second, without any kind of warning.

Check that. He had been warned, hadn't he? Warned by all the doctors, nurses and specialists.

He couldn't even bring himself to look around and see who might have observed his literal downfall. Clenching his teeth against the pain and embarrassment, he put as much weight as he could on his good leg, then used the thick base of the table to rise to a standing position.

Marni rose immediately as well and the look of worry on her face had competing forces warring in his chest. He was both touched by her concern and shamed that she'd witnessed such a stunning moment of weakness.

"Gio?"

He clenched his fists at his sides, here came that question again. *Are you all right?*

Marni didn't voice the words out loud, just continued scanning his face, her eyes imploring. He had to give her something. He thought about lying, telling her he'd tripped over some nonexistent object that was now miraculously gone or over a leg of a table. But what was the use? For one, she'd see right through the lie.

"I think I just put too much pressure on my bad leg. It'll be fine in a few moments."

Marni opened her mouth before closing it again, clearly at a loss for words.

He gestured to her middle. "Sorry about the drink. Your dress is all wet." Luckily, he'd ordered a vodka tonic for himself, at least she wouldn't have to walk around with a large stain on her dress. Just a large wet spot.

She blinked. "It will dry."

Gio finally dared to look about the room. No one seemed to be paying them any attention. If anyone had witnessed what had just happened, they had the good sense not to stare.

Still, he had to get out of this room. He didn't think he could handle even one person approaching him. "Excuse me for a few moments," he told Marni. "I'd like to get some air."

He turned away before she could respond.

Marni watched Gio's retreating back and debated what to do. Should she follow him? What if he fell again? She gave her head a small shake. No, he needed time alone and appeared steady enough on his feet as he navigated the crowded ballroom.

She would give him a minute. If she knew Gio, he was stinging with an imagined hit to his pride, which was ridiculous. He couldn't help what had just happened. He'd overdone it, pushed himself too far and ignored the fact that he wasn't one hundred percent. It had all taken a toll at the worst time.

But Gio Santino had never been one to show any weakness. And to think, Nella had said a couple days ago that he wasn't so stubborn. Ha! If she only knew just how stubborn her brother was acting these days.

A twinge of guilt fluttered in her chest. A lot of what he'd done had been on her behalf. Marni wanted to kick herself. She should have never agreed to this silly plan, should have just taken her lumps from Ander's conniving and not involved anyone else in her problems.

Along with an apology, she was going to tell Gio all that as soon as he returned.

Marni pulled her phone out of her clutch purse and mindlessly scrolled through various sites to kill the time until he returned, not paying any kind of real attention to what she read. Several moments passed and she continued scrolling.

Gio still hadn't come back. She dialed his number but he didn't pick up. No shocker there. Marni couldn't decide whether to be annoyed or more worried.

Finally, when she couldn't take any more anxious wondering, she went to look for him.

Gio wasn't in the lobby nor was he outside by the main entrance. She ran back through the lobby area and down the opposite corridor to the back of the hotel facing the beach.

Lit fire torches dotted the sand beyond a wide stone patio furnished with cushioned wicker furniture. All of the chairs and sofas sat empty.

Marni strained her eyes down the length of the beach. Countless people were walking along the water or enjoying an evening swim. It could take her hours to find Gio if he was down there. He'd had quite a head start.

A deep, masculine voice sounded behind her. "Looking for me?"

Marni clasped her hand to her chest, her heart racing. It was anybody's guess whether that was caused by Gio unexpectedly materializing from behind her or because of the figure he posed. Framed in shadows, he looked almost ethereal.

She sucked in a breath and forced her mouth to work. "Gio. There you are. You startled me."

He stepped out of the darkness into the pool of light cast from a nearby lantern. "My apologies."

She knew better than to ask him if he was all right. That had never worked out quite so well in the past.

"I'm guessing you don't want to go back into the party just yet."

He thrust his hands in his pockets, tilting backward on his heels. "You would be correct."

Good. Because neither did she. Marni stepped to the wicker seat closest to her and dropped into it, then tucked her feet under her. The fresh air felt good on her skin, the ballroom had grown much too stuffy.

Gio didn't make any kind of move to sit himself, he merely lifted an eyebrow. She couldn't help but notice that most of his weight was solidly on his good leg. Saints give her patience with this man. He thought he'd appear weak by sitting down.

Oh, Gio. You don't have to prove anything to me.

"So when are you making the call?" she asked, feeling a little disconcerted with the height difference now that she'd taken a seat and he'd remained standing.

"Call?"

"The hospital in Chicago. To schedule those appointments finally. First thing tomorrow morning, I hope."

His head tilted. "I told you a few days ago. I'm in no rush."

He couldn't be serious. But there was no sign of joking on his face. "But that was before—"

He cut her off. "I'll call when I'm ready."

Marni covered her face with her palms, hardly able to believe what she was hearing. "Gio, you need to get started on those therapy sessions. And then you need to go through the surgeries. You can't put it off any longer."

"Is that your expert opinion?"

Marni's temper flared. How could he take this so lightly? It made absolutely no sense.

"Please explain to me why you plan to put this off any longer than you already have. Especially after what just happened."

A muscle jumped along his jaw. "Nothing happened, Marni. I lost my footing. It happens to everyone."

Maybe so, but it didn't often happen while simply walking on a flat surface. "Are you trying to convince yourself of that or trying to convince me?"

He shrugged. "I don't have to convince you of anything."

Marni pushed past the hurtful barb, one meant to imply that this was none of her business. She'd deal with the wound it caused to her soul later. Right now, she really wanted to learn why Gio was doing something so harmful and dangerous to himself.

She took a deep calming breath. "I'm just trying to understand. Don't tell me you don't believe the doctors can be of help? Gio, you have to trust in the professionals who have spent their lives helping heal others."

He scoffed at that. "Of course I have faith in doctors and professionals. I'm in regular contact with Juno's medical team. I'm making sure that he gets the best care and that he's being seen by the best specialists this side of the world."

It dawned on her then. Suddenly, all the puzzle pieces fell into place and everything made sense. She'd been so wrong in all her assumptions. Gio wasn't only putting off his recovery because he was too proud to admit he was wounded. He was delaying to punish himself. For the accident he'd caused which had tragically altered the life of a young father with a family who needed him. It was a vicious circle—he refused to get the treatment he needed because of his guilt, which only grew his frustration at his injuries. He was going around and around and couldn't even see it.

"Gio, it was an accident." She emphasized the last word. "You didn't intend harm. You have to see that."

His eyes hardened on her face. "Marni, let this go."

She couldn't. For his sake. "What if I don't want to?"

His jaw visibly tightened. "It's not up to you."

She knew he was simply lashing out, but his coldness still broke her heart.

"Good night, Marni," he said in a flat voice. "The limo and speedboat are waiting to take you back to the villa whenever you're ready."

Marni's mouth went dry. He was really doing this. He was really pushing her away because he'd rather keep punishing himself than move on with his life and his future. A future that might have included *her*.

"I've decided to stay here in Naples for the time being," he added with finality.

Gio didn't even wait for a response before walking away without so much as a glance back.

Sitting in the *piazetta* sipping coffee wasn't doing much to settle her emotions. But Marni had had to get away from the villa. She'd been going stir-crazy wandering around the grounds all morning, waiting for word from Gio. The throngs of people bustling about the square and those enjoying the cafés and shops should have made for a worthy distraction of people watching. But Marni hardly noticed her surroundings.

The biscotti she'd ordered with her cappuccino was one of the freshest and most flavorful

she'd ever tasted. But she might as well have
been nibbling on cardboard.

Not a peep from him since their disastrous
argument last night. Not so much as a text or
a phone call, despite several attempts to reach
him. His silence had Marni torn between anger
and worry. What if his leg had gotten worse?
What if he was holed up in a hotel room right
now, lying on the mattress in agony and pain?

A shudder of anxiety racked through her at
the image in her head. Still, even that drastic
scenario, heaven forbid it be real, wouldn't have
prevented him from sending her a quick text.

No, he was ignoring her because he wanted
to. Because he clearly thought Marni had over-
stepped when she'd insisted he get the medical
care he needed.

Gio thought she had no right to weigh in on
his decisions. Her opinion or thought held no
import for him. And here she'd gone and fool-
ishly fallen further in love with the man. There
was no denying that now. If she couldn't admit
it before, she damn well had to face reality now.
She'd always loved him, since they were pre-
teens. Now she was head over heels.

A hiccup of anguish tore from her chest
and her eyes stung behind her sunglasses. She
reached for her phone once more, but she wasn't
holding her breath. It pinged just as she glanced

at the screen. Heart pounding, Marni unlocked the message only to have her hope plummet. It wasn't Gio but his sister.

Your plan was a success! You and Gio are all over the sites.

Marni tossed the phone back on the table as if it had burned her palm. The plan. What an insignificance. Little did Nella know she could care less now about the blasted plan. Even less about what the world thought about her. She'd take her chances to get her career back on track. If that meant leaving home and moving to New York then so be it.

Right now, regaining her professional career was pretty much all she had in her life. But she'd do it on her own terms. Without a pretend boy-friend.

One challenge at a time. For right now, she had to focus on herself and the best way to move forward toward her future.

She'd done it again—carelessly trusted her heart to the wrong man. Unlike Ander, this particular man would be impossible to get over.

Gio was the one who'd made her feel like a princess. The one who'd encouraged her to dream of more for her future and told her he had faith that she could accomplish it. He was the only man who'd sent shivers down her spine when he so much as touched her.

No matter what the future held for her, Gio Santino would forever claim her heart. All the more tragic given the family connection.

They were to be co-godparents for heaven's sake! How in the world would she even navigate that? How would she hide her true feelings and keep from shattering inside every time they were in the same room together?

With trembling fingers, she reached for her cup and took a tentative sip. Well, she was done waiting. There was no sense staying in Capri any longer either. Her goal to come here and take two weeks to recharge and regroup had completely backfired. She had nothing to show for herself but a broken heart. Looked like her days in paradise were over. Gio had clearly moved on.

Somehow, some way, so would she.

He sensed it as soon as he let himself in the front door. Gio didn't need to walk through the villa to know that she was gone. He should have answered her calls. But he couldn't bring himself to do it, couldn't for the life of him figure out what he might say. Now that he was ready to find her, it was much too late.

He knew that made him all kinds of a coward.

He'd spent hours wandering the city last night until his leg had screamed at him to stop. When he finally returned to the hotel, Gio hadn't been able to fall asleep, hadn't even bothered to crawl into bed. Just simply sat on the sofa in his hotel room, staring into the dark until the sun rose. And it had nothing to do with the regular insomnia that had plagued him since the accident.

When his eyes had finally drifted shut sometime late in the afternoon, his mind played reels of images in his head: Marni pouncing into his bedroom that first day she'd arrived; the marvel on her face as they'd sailed over blue water in the grotto; how her eyes had widened in the Gardens of Augustus... The way her lips had tasted on his.

With a curse, he strode to the patio and dropped down on the lounge chair only to have more memories of her flood his mind. He even replayed the moment in the garden when the wedding procession had walked by. Only, the bride in his mind was Marni. And he was her groom. He had to push the vision away. Because it was complete fantasy.

Maybe it was just as well she was gone. She was better off without him. He wasn't anywhere near the man he used to be.

Marni deserved better than the man he was now. Broken both inside and outside. Unable to tell the woman he loved how he really felt. Too broken for the likes of someone like her. Hopefully, one day she would see the truth of that and forgive him for his cowardness.

Heaven knew, he didn't deserve such grace from her. Just like he didn't deserve *her*.

CHAPTER THIRTEEN

Four months later

MARNI READ THE email once more, then rubbed her eyes to make sure she wasn't imagining the message. Was it really possible that they were about to be hired by their first client?

"Huh," she said out loud, scanning her laptop screen once more.

"What is it?" Nikita Murtag asked from her desk across the small office. Nikita was Marni's new business partner of approximately three weeks now. A former colleague at Marni's old firm, the other woman had contacted her the day Marni left Capri. Niki told her how low morale had turned at her old place of business. How most of the female employees knew Ander to be a predatory liar and didn't want to be next in his crosshairs. So Niki had quit. Somehow, within days after Niki's call, the two women were cosigning a business loan and painting the walls of their new shop in Boston's South End.

The signage even worked out, just as Marni had envisioned in her fantasy that night. Her mind reflexively pushed the memory aside before it could fully form. Any thoughts of the time she'd spent with Gio Santino were too painful and raw to entertain. Her heart couldn't take it.

What mattered now was that Mar-Ni Designs was officially open for business. And if this email wasn't some king of spam or junk, they might even have their first client.

"Come look at this," she told Niki, then turned the laptop toward her when the other woman reached her desk. Niki read the message over her shoulder then let out a whoop.

"We have a job!"

It certainly seemed so. "It's odd, isn't it, though?" Marni questioned. "We've barely been open more than a few days."

"Word of mouth is a powerful force, Marni. Don't discount it."

"They sent the email through the new website."

"Looks like they're asking for you specifically." Niki gave her shoulder a squeeze. "You must have impressed somebody through the years. Go ahead and confirm."

Within minutes of her replying, another message popped up.

"You're not going to believe this," she told Niki. "Whoever this potential client is, it says they're in a hurry and want a meeting this afternoon if possible."

"Are you going to say yes?" Niki asked.

Marni shrugged one shoulder. She couldn't think of one reason to turn down a potential opportunity. "Why not?" she answered. "It's not like I have anything else to work on just yet."

Three hours later, Marni made her way to the most exclusive restaurant in Boston's Seaport District, the requested meeting place, with her portfolio tucked under her arm. The dining room was relatively empty given the early afternoon so she was surprised when the maître d' led her to a private room on the top floor.

Whomever this potential client was, looked like he carried a lot of clout in the city. Marni took a seat at the large mahogany dining table, nervous anticipation humming through her veins.

A shadow fell over the table from behind her seat. A familiar scent carried in the air.

It couldn't be. Marni squeezed her eyes shut, afraid to turn around.

"Ciao, gattina."

That voice. *His* voice.

Her mind had to be playing tricks on her, trying to conjure a false reality she wanted so badly to be true. Gio Santino wasn't really here, standing behind her.

Only one way to find out.

Sucking in a shaky breath, she made herself get up and turn around.

Even as her eyes fell on him, she couldn't quite believe what she was seeing. Gio stood in the doorway, his shoulder leaning against the doorframe. He flashed her a devilishly handsome smile that made her heart skip a beat.

"Gio?"

"*Sì, bellisima.* It's me."

Marni felt as if her mouth had filled with sawdust and her tongue felt too heavy to move. Somehow she managed to form a single word. "Why?"

Gio squeezed his eyes shut, tilted his head up toward the ceiling. "You have every reason to be upset, *cara.*"

That got her mouth working. "Of course I do! You—you just left me. Without a goodbye. Not a word!"

He paused before returning his gaze to her face. "I know. For the life of me, I couldn't come up with a thing to say to you. Please know that I will spend the rest of my life trying to make up for that."

A sudden war was being waged in her soul. Every cell in her body wanted to tell him he was forgiven, that she was overjoyed to see him. But a calmer, saner part reminded her how hard she'd worked these past few months to focus solely on her own growth and fulfillment.

Whatever his intentions were for being here, she had to set him straight on at least that one thing. "You can't just walk back into my life, Gio. It's not that simple. I've done a lot since we last saw each other."

He took a step closer, his eyes dark and compelling beneath those black lashes.

Focus.

"I know. From all outward appearances, it seems your new business is exactly what you'd envisioned. You should be so proud of yourself."

Her chin lifted. "I am. And I don't have room or time to waste if my feelings are one-sided."

Gio moved closer to her once more. Something nagged at the back of her mind when he took several more steps. It took a beat, but she finally figured out what her brain was trying to tell her. "Your limp," she began. "It seems to be better."

He gave her a thin smile. "It should. After the countless hours of therapy and all the grueling muscle building exercises."

Marni sucked in a breath. "You went to Chicago."

He nodded.

"You were right to push me that night. And I was so wrong to push you away. I'm so sorry, *mi gattina*. Please forgive me for being such a *stolto*."

She couldn't help herself, didn't even realize what she'd intended until she was across the room and in his arms. He wrapped himself around her, nuzzled his chin against the top of her head.

"You're really here," she said against his chest, savoring the feel of him, inhaling deeply of that scent she'd missed so much.

"I had to come. To find the woman I love."

The woman he loved? If this was indeed a dream, Marni didn't want to ever come back to reality. Gio Santino had traveled across the country to be with her, to tell her he loved her.

But there were so many things as yet unsettled. She couldn't celebrate until she had the answers she'd been asking for that night in Naples. Marni made herself pull away. "What about your treatments?" If she was remembering correctly, he still had surgeries to complete after the therapy was over. "Don't you have to go back to Chicago for the surgeries?"

He tilted her chin. "Chicago is so far, *mi amore*."

She was about to argue when he pressed a finger to her lips. "I'm already seeing a specialist. Right here in Boston. I refuse to be so far from you again. I intend to stay right here and do all I can to work on becoming the man you deserve."

Marni thought her heart might burst in her chest. Then she couldn't think at all as his lips found hers.

When he pulled away all too soon, he took her by the hand to the table. "Now, let's get down to business, shall we?"

Marni blinked at him in confusion. "What business?"

He chuckled. "You're here about an assignment, aren't you?"

Marni didn't miss the mischief behind his eyes. What was he getting at?

"I thought that was just a ruse to get me here." As if she'd turn him down if he'd just asked her. He couldn't have really thought so.

He shook his head. "No ruse. There's a property that needs a professional decorator. As a fan of your previous work, I believe you'd be perfect for the job."

Marni tilted her head, whatever game he was playing, she'd play along. "What property?"

"Here, let me show you." He reached for a leather binder sitting in the center of the table, pulled it toward her and lifted the cover.

Marni knew immediately what she was looking at. "This is the villa in Capri. The one that was for sale." He must have bought it.

She looked more carefully at the photos and paperwork. "There's a mistake here," she said, pointing at one of the documents. "This has my name listed as the owner."

Gio flashed her a wide smile. "No mistake. The villa is yours."

Before Marni could so much as absorb that bit of information, he continued, "Consider it a wedding present for my new wife. That's if she'll have it." He took her hand in his over the table. "And if she'll have me. What do you say?"

Marni thought her heart might burst in her chest with joy. It had nothing to do with any villa. And everything to do with the man she'd loved for as long as she could remember.

"*Sì, mi amore,*" she answered, wrapping her arms around his neck. "I say yes!"

EPILOGUE

U<small>NLIKE THE LAST</small> time they were here at the Gardens of Augustus, the sky was dark and overcast. In fact, it appeared as if it might rain any second. But none of that hampered the joy flooding through her heart and soul.

Let it rain, Marni thought. An all-out thunderstorm would not be enough to dampen the celebration of her wedding day by so much as even a fraction.

As she approached the man who would soon be her husband, Marni fought the urge to pinch herself to prove all of this was real. Gio stood beneath a circular archway of flowers, the view of the ocean behind him. He looked so devastatingly handsome, his eyes shining with so much love that Marni thought her heart might burst in her chest. His sister stood next to him, beaming. Cradled in her arms was Marni's infant goddaughter, surely the cutest flower girl to have ever been in a wedding. The grand view of the Faraglioni rocks framed them.

Marni's eyes stung with happy tears. She was surrounded by love and affection and everyone who'd ever mattered in her life. The Santinos had always been her family. Now it was simply official.

Her tears refused to be contained as she reached Gio's side and they began their vows. Marni felt like she was living a true fairy tale, right down to marrying her own prince.

Afterward, through a blur of happy emotion as they began posing for their wedding photos, Gio gently took her elbow. He leaned in to whisper in her ear after the photographer snapped several pictures. "I've been thinking, *cara*. Something has occurred to me and I can't seem to get it out of my head."

Marni couldn't help but giggle at the clearly exaggerated mock seriousness in his voice. "What thought might that be, dear husband?" She had to suppress a cry of glee at the last word as it left her lips.

"I was thinking how much little Alexandra would appreciate a cousin to play with. Wouldn't you agree?"

Marni gave him a useless shove on his upper arm. "Gio!"

The photographer was trying to direct them in another pose but it was so hard to process the man's direction. She was utterly, wholeheartedly focused on her new husband.

Gio continued, "As responsible godparents, it behooves us to give our little niece all that she may desire."

"Anything you say, my love."

His expression turned suddenly serious. The photographer had apparently given up at this point and stepped to the side to wait patiently before continuing.

"Of course, the timing is entirely up to you," Gio told her. "I know you're quite busy with your growing clientele back in Boston."

"I am quite busy," she said, just to tease him.

He tapped her playfully on the nose, then dropped a soft kiss on her lips. "That's fine. Just gives me something to look forward to."

Marni cupped his face in her hands and rose on her toes to give him a deeper, longer kiss. She felt breathless and heady when they finally pulled away.

"Me too, my love," she whispered against his lips. "I'm looking forward to all of it. All that we have in front of us."

* * * * *